Dear Reader,

I have to admit, I'm pretty much in love with my hero, Gabriel Black. He's a charming bad boy with a few questionable habits (well, he *is* a con man), but he has a heart of gold and a penchant for rescuing people—especially damsels in distress. If there is ever a woman who can take care of herself, it's FBI special agent Danita Cruz. These were such fun characters to put together, because they are both so vulnerable, yet so good at hiding it—even from themselves. I hope you enjoy reading about their sensual adventures as much as I loved writing them.

This book featured a special guest, too—Pippi the cat, who lives at Furry Friends Animal Shelter. You can check out Pippi, and all the other Blaze Authors Pet Project pets, on the Blaze authors blog—http://blazeauthors.com. Please, come by and say hi! And if you're on the web, be sure to drop by my website, www.tawnyweber.com.

Happy Valentine's Day!

Tawny Weber

Tawny Weber

SEX, LIES AND VALENTINES

Chrysti Riehl
Box 185
Wildwood AB T0E 2M0
(780) 325-2119

TORONTO NEW YORK LONDON
AMSTERDAM PARIS SYDNEY HAMBURG
STOCKHOLM ATHENS TOKYO MILAN MADRID
PRAGUE WARSAW BUDAPEST AUCKLAND

Recycling programs
for this product may
not exist in your area.

ISBN-13: 978-0-373-79670-0

SEX, LIES AND VALENTINES

Copyright © 2012 by Tawny Weber

ABOUT THE AUTHOR

Tawny Weber is usually found dreaming up stories in her California home, surrounded by dogs, cats and kids. When she's not writing hot, spicy stories for the Harlequin Blaze line, she's shopping for the perfect pair of shoes or drooling over Johnny Depp pictures (when her husband isn't looking, of course). Come by and visit her on the web at www.tawnyweber.com or on Facebook at www.facebook.com/TawnyWeber.RomanceAuthor.

Books by Tawny Weber

HARLEQUIN BLAZE

324—DOUBLE DARE
372—DOES SHE DARE?
418—RISQUÉ BUSINESS
462—COMING ON STRONG
468—GOING DOWN HARD
492—FEELS LIKE THE FIRST TIME
513—BLAZING BEDTIME STORIES, VOLUME III
    "You Have to Kiss a Lot of Frogs..."
564—RIDING THE WAVES
579—IT MUST HAVE BEEN THE MISTLETOE...
    "A Babe in Toyland"
592—BREAKING THE RULES
612—JUST FOR THE NIGHT
656—SEX, LIES AND MISTLETOE
660—SEX, LIES AND MIDNIGHT

To get the inside scoop on Harlequin Blaze and its talented writers, be sure to check out blazeauthors.com.

Don't miss any of our special offers. Write to us at the following address for information on our newest releases.

Harlequin Reader Service
U.S.: 3010 Walden Ave., P.O. Box 1325, Buffalo, NY 14269
Canadian: P.O. Box 609, Fort Erie, Ont. L2A 5X3

To Jeanne Adams, as a thank you for answering my plea for help. Over and over and over. You rock!!

Prologue

"YOU'RE PUSHING your luck. If you're not careful, you'll lose everything you've worked for, including your freedom."

Contemplating that, Tobias Black leaned back in his leather chair, looking out the window at his kingdom—otherwise known as the small town of Black Oak. Then he sighed and glanced toward his speaker phone.

"Some things are worth the risk, my friend. Having my family back is one of them."

"Have you ever considered simply calling your son, asking him to come home and help you?" Exasperation rang through the phone like a bell. "You're under investigation for multiple criminal activities. The man who was attacked in your own motorcycle shop not three weeks ago has accused you not only of the act, but as being the leader of a new crime conglomerate forming in Northern California. And instead of focusing on clearing your name, you're plotting to con your own son."

"Not con," Tobias corrected meticulously. "I don't do cons anymore, remember? I've reformed and made restitution for everything I stole over the years."

"That won't stop you from being convicted if you don't

clear your name. Is it worth the risk to play such an elaborate game?"

Tobias considered that question. Two months ago, he'd dealt this hand and won in spades. Not only had he pulled the strings to bring his oldest son, Caleb, home, the boy was now town sheriff and getting married.

A month ago, counting on his daughter Maya's determination to save him from himself, he'd dealt the next hand. That one had been a winner, too. But barely, considering Maya had brought her very own FBI agent home with her. The game had gotten dicey there for a while. But that only added to the pleasure of winning. And winning in that case meant Maya was moving back to town, and engaged to be married.

Now he had to deal with Gabriel.

Of his three children, Gabriel was the one who was most like Tobias himself. This would be his biggest challenge. Tobias felt his stomach clench. Nerves? He'd once conned a former U.S. President into supporting a fraudulent charity and had only felt glee. But facing his family, initiating this last stage of the game… Big winged moths were battling in his belly.

"It's worth the risk," he repeated as if he wasn't worried. "Even if I begged, Gabriel wouldn't come home. This is the only way to get him here. We need someone on the inside. Someone with a reputation that will convince the criminals that he's one of them. But more importantly, someone with a vested interest in clearing my name."

"And you truly believe the criminal contingent meeting there in town will let him in?"

"Thanks to Caleb's research, we know three of the crime bosses' names. I've made arrangements with someone whose computer skills I trust."

That someone being his daughter, who was gifted with amazing hacking skills. He took a deep breath, knowing he was committed to this. He had to be; his freedom, his family, his very life depended on it. But it was the hardest thing he'd ever done.

"This someone hacked their email using mirror accounts, so each of them thinks the other is putting Gabriel's name forth as the last member. They've taken the bait, and his invitation has been issued from whoever is leading this scheme."

Even as he said the words, a fission of fear worked its way down his spine. It was one thing to conceive a con, to hone the details. Even to set the game in motion. But to bring his son home meant putting him in the arms of criminals who, unlike Tobias, had no compunction in using violence. He was risking a lot for himself. But he was risking just as much for his son.

"Fine, fine. As usual, you've crafted an intricate net that will undoubtedly get the results you want." The other man sighed, then added in a tone of someone who knew he'd be ignored. "But having your own son arrested in order to get him home might be taking it a step too far, old friend. Even for you."

1

GABRIEL BLACK LEANED back against the rich teak of the bar and smiled with satisfaction. At his elbow was a glass of the finest aged Scotch. His suit was Armani, his shoes were Ferragamo and his shirt was silk. In his pocket was the key to millions in internet stocks.

Not bad for a Thursday night.

A natural born gambler, he had a talent for winning. And he had a feeling that tonight's win was gonna be a big one.

"Buy me a drink?"

He glanced over and offered the pouty redhead with a set of dangerous curves a long look. With a flick of his finger, he motioned to the bartender to bring her whatever she wanted. As Moe placed a flute of champagne next to her, Gabriel offered a charming smile and tilted his head toward the men who'd just walked in the door.

"I've got a few things to take care of," he told the redhead. With one eye still on the mark, he leaned over and ran the back of his index finger along the shoulder left bare by her strapless glittery dress. "Enjoy your champagne, keep my seat warm and when I'm finished we'll take the rest of that bottle back to my room."

"I'll look forward to that," she purred, touching the tip of her tongue to the crystal flute before sliding onto the velvet covered barstool.

For just one second, Gabriel was distracted. He leaned over and took the glass from her, twisted it to drink from the same place her lips had been, marked by a crimson smear of lipstick. The champagne exploded on his tongue. Just like he figured the sex would later.

"Tasty," he murmured, handing back the glass.

With a quick wink, he turned away and scanned the room. Instantly, his gaze found his mark and his partner settling into a booth in the corner.

Just like that, the redhead was as good as gone in his mind. One of Gabriel's strengths was his ability to ignore anything that stood between him and his goal. And as much as he adored women, they had their place. In his bed, against the wall, rising over his nude body. Those were all good places. But no woman had ever entered his mind when he was on a job.

After all, the job was everything.

A little something he'd learned from his old man. But as amazing as Tobias Black was, he had never quite managed to master that one particular rule. Gabriel's father was king of the con, but he'd never let go of emotional ties. That'd been his downfall, and the reason he was now out of the game.

Gabriel admired his old man's skills. But he was better.

But he'd wait to gloat until later. After he'd relieved these gentleman of a cool mil.

He knew the affable smile on his face didn't detract from the air of danger he wore like a second skin. But, whether it was in a professional poker game or while pulling a con, the elegant suit and five-hundred-dollar haircut fooled people long enough for him to get the job done.

"Gentlemen," he greeted when he reached their booth. With a nod to each man, he pulled up a chair.

"Mr. Lane," the first man greeted, using Gabriel's false identity. Hair slicked back from an unfortunate face, he was the kind of guy you just knew had been picked on all through high school. The dateless kind who'd focused all that teenage sexual frustration on studying so he could make the kind of money that bought plenty of admiration.

"We're glad you agreed to meet us," the second guy said. This one was more wary. The accountant, he was here to make sure his friend didn't get hosed.

Good. Anything that came too easily was boring. Gabriel believed in working for his money. And he hated to be bored.

"I appreciate you agreeing to meet here," Gabriel said, nodding his head to the hotel's private bar. "I've been called away on a sudden trip to Europe. If we couldn't do this tonight, it would have to wait until I get back in two weeks. I don't mind waiting, of course. This deal is only getting sweeter. But you're good guys and I hate to delay your buy in."

"I've looked over your prospectus and the terms of the sale," the accountant started to say. Then his eyes widened and he seemed to lose track. Gabriel followed his gaze and damn near swallowed his tongue.

Hello, baby.

The room faded. The deal was a distant memory.

Like a laser, his focus honed in on the blonde.

She was straight out of every man's fantasy. Big curls spiraled around a face that screamed hot sex. Eyes so blue they were almost purple flashed, the long lush lashes and smudged makeup giving her the look of a very satisfied woman who'd just slipped out of a rumpled bed. One where she'd left a very satisfied man smiling with exhaustion.

The curls teased shoulders, bare except for glitter and a tiny set of black straps. Gabriel eyed those straps and his mouth went dry. Her breasts were perfect. Black fabric, as glittery as her skin, cupped the rounded globes like a lover's hands. His gaze followed the glitter to a waist small enough for him to span with both hands. Black leather wrapped around her hips, giving way to long—oh, baby, they were so gloriously long—legs. His gaze finished the tour at her feet and Gabriel hoped like hell he wasn't drooling.

Her shoes were mostly ribbon, tied in a sassy bow at her ankle. High, spiked and black, they were the kind of shoes meant to be worn with a light gloss of body lotion and nothing else.

He dragged his eyes back up to her face.

Her mouth was wet and glossy, the lower lip full and tempting. A tiny dimple played out as she shot Gabriel an inviting look.

As her date, a guy who was just a blur to Gabriel, pulled out her chair, she seemed to melt into it in a single, sinuous move. Her eyes still locked on his, she offered Gabriel a tiny wink and blew him a kiss.

Gabriel's body went on high alert. High passion alert, that was. Muscles tense, his stomach clenched in anticipation. His fingers itched to touch that skin. To slide his fingers over the silky expanse of bare flesh. Would she shiver? If he took her against the wall, would she wrap those long legs around his waist and hold on tight?

Everything else in the room faded.

Unlike the redhead, this wasn't a woman you put out of your mind.

Pure sex, with a dangerously sweet edge, she had a body meant to make men beg.

And she was with someone else.

Not that he cared.

Gabriel always got what he wanted.

And he wanted her.

The only question was, how long until he had her?

Someone cleared his throat.

"Mr. Lane?"

He watched the blonde thank the waiter for her glass of iced water. Lifting it to her lips, her gaze met Gabriel's again.

He watched her throat move as she swallowed.

His body hardened.

She lowered the glass. Her eyes still locked on his, she licked one glistening drop of water off her lower lip. Soft and pink, he imagined her tongue licking other things.

And damn near groaned.

"Mr. Lane?"

Shit. He was here to do a job.

Playtime would have to come later.

Gabriel dragged his eyes off the gorgeous blonde and focused on the men in front of him. He could still see the sexy distraction out of the corner of his eye as he listened to the accountant outline his concerns about the deal. Jerry, the unfortunate-faced mark, split his attention between staring over Gabriel's shoulder and absently nodding along with his buddy.

Trying to stay focused on the game, Gabriel ignored the flash of color and light in the corner of the eye. Then Jerry winced, a shocked look crossing his homely face.

Gabriel turned his head just in time to see Blondie's date grab her by the hair.

"What the…"

Gabriel was half out of his seat when the guy pulled her mouth to his. She leaned in, like she was liking it. No struggle, no sign that she was in trouble. When he pulled away, she said something, patting the guy's chest. The smile she offered him was big and sweet.

His nerve endings raw from zigzagging between lust and the rescue-the-distressed-damsel adrenaline rush, Gabriel clenched his fist and sucked in a deep breath.

Settling in his chair, he shifted so he couldn't watch the show any longer.

He had to focus, dammit.

The priority was the game. The money.

Never a woman.

"I understand your concerns," he told the men, focusing on Jerry. He went on to outline why their thinking was wrong, and why his deal was the greatest thing invented since internet porn. It only took a few seconds before both men were nodding along, big smiles on their faces.

Not because he was so damned good, either. Nope, the guys' attention was still split, half of it on the Gabriel's pitch, the rest on the blonde over his shoulder.

Hell, he thought as he pushed the contract toward Jerry to read and sign. She was making this way too easy for him. He was starting to feel like he should offer her up a pretty sparkle or two as a thank-you for doing half his work for him.

Offering Jerry his pen and a charming smile, Gabriel could almost feel the million dollars sliding into his pocket.

Then there was a loud crash of glass hitting the floor, a muffled cry of pain and a growl and the sound of flesh hitting flesh. The room went silent for a heartbeat before the air was filled with gasps and protests.

Fury propelled Gabriel to his feet. Before he could take a step, though, the blonde gave a quick, worried shake of her head. Her face, one cheek glowing red from that asshole's hand, looked terrified.

Stay out of it, her big blue eyes begged.

A man who strongly believed in people's right to screw themselves up, Gabriel forced himself to sit back down.

He watched a busboy rush over to clean up the broken glass. Two waiters scurried, one for the table, the other probably for the manager.

Let it go, Black.

It was being taken care of. No reason for him to interfere. Or worse, to blow this deal.

He watched the blonde assure the concerned waiter that she was okay. Her date, the prick, just glared at the guy, his hand fisted around her slender arm.

Nope. He wasn't going to be able to ignore it.

Gabriel grimaced. Then, unable to help himself, he held up one finger to stop the accountant's pitch.

"Hang on," he murmured. He rose, his eyes locked on the guy bullying the pretty blonde. He stepped toward the booth, a charming warning teetering on the tip of his tongue.

The guy's beady rat eyes met Gabriel's for a brief second before he grabbed a handful of the blonde's curls and yanked again. "I'm paying you for a good time, I want a good time. You do me, girly. Here. Now," he growled.

Her quiet cry of pain was eclipsed by the red flush of humiliation warming those alabaster cheeks. She didn't look toward Gabriel any longer. Instead she whispered something, tried to pull away.

"No party, no pay," the guy responded, not whispering.

She was a rental fantasy?

Didn't matter.

Fury propelled him forward. Before she could cry out again, Gabriel had his hand around the guy's neck.

"Oh, no," the blonde moaned, her fingers reaching and missing as Gabriel yanked the guy to his feet. "Please."

His fist cocked back, Gabriel made the mistake of looking at her. Those big blue eyes, so sexy and afraid, pleaded. "Please. Let him go."

His fingers itched. His arm vibrated with the force of his fury. He wanted to plow into the man's face. To make him pay for hurting her. For humiliating her.

It was that last part, the humiliation, that made Gabriel swallow the edgy violence pounding through his system. He glared into the asshole's beady eyes and gave him a good shake before letting go.

"Out."

The jerk looked like he was going to say something. He shot the blonde a glare, then opened his mouth. Gabriel flexed his fingers. The guy ran.

"I have to…" Her face on fire as she looked around at all the staring faces, the blonde pressed one hand against those ripe, glossy lips as if holding back a sob, then got to her feet and ran from the room, too.

Torn between ambition and a desperate need to protect, Gabriel wanted to howl with fury. But, really, there was no choice. Barely sparing a glance for his mark and the million he was kissing off, Gabriel followed.

He caught her just outside the hotel, near the garden entrance.

"Hold up," he demanded, lengthening his stride to catch her before she rounded the corner. How the hell did she move so fast on those heels? Almost running now, Gabriel snagged her arm.

Her gasp was a watery protest. She yanked away, but faced him. "Don't," she said, tears pouring from those sultry blue eyes. One of those girl things or the miracle of the paint manufactures, her makeup didn't budge under all that wet. So instead of looking bruised and messy, she glowed.

Gabriel cursed under his breath. There shouldn't be anything appealing about a bawling woman.

"You shouldn't have followed me," she murmured, brushing the tips of her fingers over her face as if that'd hide her tears. She looked like she wanted to jump out of her own skin, her eyes skipping to the left, then right, before meeting his briefly then dropping somewhere in the vicinity of his shoulder.

She was even sexier close-up. Her hair glinted gold and

bright in the reflection of the streetlight. Despite her sexy outfit and wild look, she seemed delicate, almost fragile outside.

And still so freaking sexy his mouth watered for just one taste. Of those lips, glistening and full. That skin, so silky and tempting. But most of all, those curves, barely hidden by the barely-there black fabric.

"I don't rescue damsels then let them run off still distressed," Gabriel told her with a charming, patient sort of smile.

"Why?" She backed up a step, holding her hands over her breasts as if protecting her modesty. Or herself. "What do you want?"

"I'm not asking for anything," he assured her.

Skepticism etched on her face, she gave him a long, searching look.

Gabriel tried to look as innocent and harmless as possible. Not an easy task since he'd never been either.

Then she threw herself into his arms.

"Aww, sweetheart, don't cry," Gabriel murmured. He wrapped his arm around her slender shoulder and hugged her to him.

Her body fit against his perfectly. For all her delicate looks, she was tall enough to curve her cheek into his throat, her body shaking with sobs as she burrowed closer.

Damsel in distress, he reminded himself as his blood heated. He'd been called a lot of things in his life, but the kind of guy who took advantage of abused, vulnerable women didn't make the list.

Then she slid a foot along his calf. A foot that was wrapped in those sexy ribbons she probably called shoes.

Gabriel swore he felt his brain stutter. His body, already on high alert, funneled all his blood straight down to his dick.

A dick that was only too happy to have her press even closer, so her leather-clad hips made it clear where the party was.

"I needed that money," she sniffed, looking up at him with the biggest, bluest eyes he'd ever seen. Swimming in tears, the lushly lashed gaze was hypnotic, tugging at his soul. "I can't make rent without it. I'm already two weeks overdue and going to be kicked out in the morning."

All she needed was to throw in a sick grandma and an ailing cat. But still, what's a guy to do?

"Here," he said, reaching into his pocket, then peeling four hundreds out of his wallet. "This will cover your loss. Now let's go in and dry your tears. I'll buy you a drink, then get you a cab ride home."

She gave a shuddering breath. The kind that pressed those delicate breasts against his chest

"Thank you," she whispered after a brief hesitation. She gave him a look that was somewhere between gratitude and pure seduction. Gabriel was pretty sure he heard a few of his brain cells explode in tiny little sexual pops. "But I can't take your money. Not unless you let me thank you. Properly."

His brain fogged with an edgy, needy passion, Gabriel tried to find the words to tell her he didn't need to be thanked.

Before he could, though, she slid her hands, palms flat, up his chest. Smoothing, but not soothing. Heating his skin through the layers of fabric as easily as if he'd been nude.

As she curled her hands around the back of his neck, she leaned in, her breasts amping that heat up to a fiery level.

Gabriel's hands curved over her leather-slick hips, pulling her closer, tighter.

Her mouth met his. Soft at first, just the brush of those glossy lips. Once, then twice.

Sweet.

She slanted her head to the side. Their lips fit together perfectly. Too perfectly for his comfort, he realized. Shifting, he prepared to pull back. Then she slid her tongue along the seam of his mouth and what was left of his brains spontaneously combusted.

The kiss went wild. Tongues slid over each other. No soft caress here—it was an intense duel for control. Hot, intense.

Fabulous.

Before Gabriel could take it a little hotter, a little wilder, she pulled back. Her eyes were huge. Passion, and something that looked like a cross between fear and horror, swam in those blue depths.

Then she blinked and looked sultry again.

"That's just a taste of my thank-you," she purred.

"I'm looking forward to another bite," he murmured, lowering his head to try her again.

"Put your hands on your head," a voice barked from behind Gabriel.

He could barely hear through the roaring in his head. Everything he was, everything he had, was focused on the blonde and the sexual desperation she was spinning in his body.

"You heard me. Back away, mister," the voice sounded again.

"What?" His fingers still burning with the feel of her, delicately tempting, Gabriel curled them into her shoulders to shield her from the interruption. The blonde, though, gave a shuddering sigh, then stepped back and made a show of slipping the cash into her bodice.

"Hands on your head." The voice, male and angry, was doing serious damage to the passion buzzing through his system.

Before Gabriel could decide what to do about it, hell, before he could reengage his brain, someone grabbed him.

"What the hell..."

The distinct rattle of handcuffs filled the air just before the metal slapped against Gabriel's wrist.

"You're under arrest for solicitation."

"Are you freakin' kidding me?" Gabriel tried to wrench his arm free. But even at six-three, he was no match for the hairy gorilla with a badge glaring down at him.

His gaze cut to the blonde.

Her gaze didn't glow with tears, or passion any longer.

Nope, she just looked satisfied.

Gabriel resisted the urge to cuss.

Because he was damned sure she was the only one of the two of them who'd be feeling any satisfaction tonight.

"WE BOTH KNOW you don't have a case against me. Which means I'm here as a courtesy," Gabriel stated in a bored tone as he leaned back in a surprisingly comfortable chair. He stared at the guy who had to be a cop, even though he hadn't introduced himself. Nor had anyone trotted out the Miranda, and they weren't in a copshop, yet. So this was about something else. "Why don't you tell me what you want, and then I can be on my way."

For all his cocky tone, a niggling of worry tickled the back of Gabriel's neck. But he brushed it aside. His ID claimed him as Gavin Lane. Even though he hadn't planned to, he'd left the incriminating paperwork at the hotel with Jerry. He wasn't worried. They had nothing on him.

Despite his lack of concern, the way the other guy—was he a cop?—was ignoring him was starting to get irritating.

"Entrapment never looks good to the brass, you know. Add to that, I didn't agree to pay the babe for sex. So why don't we do both ourselves a favor and call it a night."

The guy didn't respond. He just kept on flipping through some fat file folder.

His jaw as tight as the muscles bunched in his shoulders, Gabriel was starting to get seriously pissed.

Being ignored had a way of doing that to him.

"So…"

Finally, the guy said something.

As he spoke, the cop—or whatever the hell he was—finished reading the file, then set it on the desk. This was a guy who was into control, Gabriel decided. Not the best adversary considering he also held most of the cards. But Gabriel's daddy had taught him at a young age to keep an ace or two up his sleeve, so he was confident he'd get through this. It was just another game.

"I'm Hunter," introduced the man. He didn't offer to shake hands, though. Just as well, since his name was ringing some bells. Warning bells, that is.

There had been a guy by the name of Hunter who'd spent a good portion of his FBI career chasing Gabriel's old man. Narrowing his eyes, Gabe inspected the man in front of him. Mid-thirties, at the most. Local law, not federal, right? He'd have flashed credentials if he was a feebie.

The name was just a coincidence.

Spend enough time committing crime, and sooner or later a guy had to start doubling up on names. Law of averages and all that.

Relaxing into the chair again, Gabriel offered a cocky smile and said, "Nice to meet you, Hunter. Now maybe you can explain what, exactly, is going on here."

Hunter leaned back in his chair with a long, considering look. But he didn't say a word.

He didn't have to.

His body language, the look on his face, the very air around him, they all said trouble.

Gabriel almost grinned.

This guy was good.

Anticipation zinged through him. A nice rush of excitement that'd make the irritation of retrieving his deal all the sweeter.

His cover was rock solid. A solicitation charge?

Brow arched, Gabriel leaned back in the chair, crossed his ankle over his knee and waited, too.

He loved this moment. Those few seconds just before the win. He could taste the victory.

A door opened behind him. Gabriel didn't take his gaze off Hunter's though. They were the real players in this game, nobody else mattered.

Perfume teased his senses. Something fresh. Light. It shouldn't have tapped into his desire, and yet his body stirred.

Then she came around, standing next to Hunter's side of the desk. Shoulders back, arms loose at her sides, she clearly stood at attention.

Shit.

Gabriel's body warred with itself, passion punched him in the gut even as contemptuous irritation stirred.

Instead of teased out in wild curls, her blond hair was slicked back in a tidy ponytail reminiscent of the Barbie Gabriel's sister used to carry around.

He noted with regret that instead of barely covered in glitter and a few strips of shiny fabric, those tempting breasts were now demurely hidden by a crisp white blouse, the wide collar framing her face. Paired with the gunmetal gray skirt that hugged her from hips to knees and a pair of pointy toed black heels, the look screamed business.

He missed the sexy business her other outfit had screamed. Uptight do-gooders were irritating and unappealing.

So why did he find her as hot now as he had when she was all tarted up?

"I believe you've met Special Agent Danita Cruz," Hunter introduced with the slightest inclination of his head.

Special Agent?

The tiny hairs on the back of his neck stood on end. That, and the warning buzz going off in his head, said this game had just taken a turn for the worse.

His worse.

As if reading his mind, Hunter's lips twitched. Then he inclined his head toward Gabriel as the blonde stationed herself on Hunter's left.

She looked like the cat who was about to nibble on a canary. Gabriel shifted so both feet were flat on the floor. Defensive position, yes. But the warning buzz was getting louder. And women didn't get that cocky without a really good reason.

Maybe he wasn't going to wiggle out of everything quite as easily as he'd thought.

Then Hunter said, "Danita, this is Gabriel Black."

He shot Gabriel a smug smile, just this side of cocky, and leaned back in his chair before adding, "He's going to help us close the Black Oak case."

2

Danita Cruz had one goal in life.

To prove she wasn't the worthless piece of trash she'd been called so often in her early years.

She'd grown up with her mother holding the title as the meanest drunk in the trailer park. When Mom hadn't been wasted, she'd specialized in petty drug deals and moving stolen goods. Danita's childhood had been a revolving door of lowlife scum. Not a promising beginning. And one that Danita might not have crawled out of if not for Hunter. She'd only been fifteen when he'd busted her mother for her part in a carjacking ring. He'd locked away the boogie man, then he'd dared her to dream of life beyond her miserable past. He'd become a friend, a mentor and a nagging big brother all rolled into one.

She owed him everything.

She'd worked hard to get where she was in the FBI. She'd busted her ass to put herself through college, to put all traces of her past behind her. To build a life she could be proud of. To craft a reputation as a smart, savvy and dependable agent who followed the book and got the job done.

She glared across the room. And now this criminal, this

conniving con artist, was giving her a look filled with contempt. Like she was somehow dirty.

Two hours ago, he'd been looking at her like she was his every fantasy come true. Those intense molten gold eyes had glowed with appreciation. Now they just stared with chilly disdain.

Ignoring that, she studied the face she'd seen plenty of times in surveillance photos. Elegant angles, sleek cheekbones and long-lidded eyes that made her insides want to melt. Reputedly a gambler who traveled the world following the game, the man screamed class, from the tip of his expensively styled black hair to the toes of his designer shoes.

Obviously in Gabriel Black's case, class was easily purchased. Just like his dates.

"Danita, have a seat," Hunter invited.

She didn't want to sit. Suddenly, she didn't want to be here at all. But running from the room, and away from those molten gold eyes that were staring holes right through her, was chicken. As was ignoring an order, however politely it'd been worded.

So she sat, angling her body toward Hunter as if she were dismissing the other man. Her body was painfully aware of him, though. Just being in the same room brought back the same hot, sticky need that he'd inspired when he'd kissed her.

A need she'd just as tidily ignored as she was ignoring the man who'd inspired it. Resolute, Danita squared her shoulders and tried to focus on Hunter and the case.

"I'm sure you're wondering why we went to so much trouble to bring you here," he was saying. "And you're probably thinking this solicitation charge is trumped-up bullshit, easy to get out of."

"Two for two," Black said, his tone amused. But Danita caught the fury layered beneath that smooth surface. "You want something from me, obviously. And want it badly enough to send Blondie as bait."

"My name is Danita," she snapped. "Or better yet, Special Agent Cruz."

"Babe, to me you'll always be the hot blonde with a body that won't quit and lips made for men's fantasies."

An angry red haze heated Danita's glare. A nasty rejoinder was on the tip of her lips before she caught herself.

What was wrong with her? She was a smart, savvy woman who'd built a name by using all the tools at her disposal to great, often devastating effect.

She'd taken the detriments and scars of her childhood—the lousy upbringing, humiliating reputation and exposure to the miserable side of life—and twisted it all in her favor.

And thanks to those tools, including the idiot-inducing reaction men had to her looks and her body, had helped solidify her case closure rate at a tidy ninety-eight percent. She was damned good.

So why did she care what Gabriel Black thought of her? The man was a criminal, for crying out loud.

With that in mind, instead of snapping at him again, she leaned back in her chair and offered haughty look of disdain.

"What I want is to offer you an opportunity," Hunter said, picking up the conversation thread Danita had almost let Black break with his mouthy remark.

"Why?"

"In part, because I believe you can be helpful to a little project of mine," Hunter told him. Then he shrugged and offered a ghost of a smile. "And in part because we have a mutual…friend, shall we say, who'd appreciate me cutting you a little slack."

Confusion furrowed her brow. What was going on?

Despite their history, Hunter was her boss. And he operated his task force on a need-to-know basis. So all Danita had been given when she was briefed that afternoon was the name of their quarry and the fact that the case was titled Black Oak. A woman who believed in being prepared, she'd pulled up Gabriel Black's file. Most of it was under a confidential lock, but she'd gotten the basics: Gabriel Black was a suspected con artist with a talent for sliding out of trouble. She'd assumed Hunter planned to use the man as a tool to bust his father.

Her gaze bounced between the two men as she tried to get a handle on this shift. Because it wasn't sounding at all like a trap to her. There was something else going on.

"Here's the deal. We have you on a minor charge. To you, it's an inconvenience." Hunter paused long enough for the other man to nod. Danita noticed Black didn't look cocky anymore. His eyes were narrow with suspicion, his brow furrowed and fingers tapping an irritated rhythm on his knee. Smart man.

"Inconveniences are a tricky thing, though," Hunter continued. "Sometimes they are easily swept away. And sometimes they blow up into something bigger. Something more long-term. Five to seven years long."

The tapping stopped. Black leaned forward, both hands flat on his thighs. "You don't have anything worth five to seven."

"Actually, I do. Those internet security documents you left at the hotel, along with the contract the gentleman enthusiastically signed, are easily worth at least that long."

"It sounds like you have enough to get my attention. But not my cooperation." Black leaned back, both brows arched as he waited.

"Oh, I have a little more."

"Do tell."

"Tobias, Caleb and Maya," Hunter said, drawing out the names like a man who knew he'd just played a winning hand.

If the stunned look on Gabriel's face was anything to go by, those names were the jackpot. A jackpot he hadn't expected—and didn't want to lose.

"You don't have anything on them," he said. His words were quiet. But there was a deadly fury beneath them. Danita's breath lodged in her throat and her body tensed, as if she'd have to break up a vicious fistfight any second now.

"I have a witness who is willing to testify about Tobias Black's role in running illegal arms and drugs. The FBI has compiled a solid case and we're ready to proceed without your cooperation."

Black's jaw worked. The same eyes that had looked at her so tenderly earlier were furious slits. Finally he arched one brow and asked, "What's that to do with Caleb and Maya?"

Danita looked at Hunter, looking forward to his answer. Instead of saying anything, though, he lifted a file off his desk and handed it to the man across from him. Black held his gaze as he took it, then slowly, lowered his eyes and read.

The man was good. Damned good. His expression didn't change. But Danita could tell that the file was freaking him out. When he was finished, he didn't hand it back to Hunter. Instead he flicked the edges like it was nothing, and gave her boss a bored look.

"So you've found a few past indiscretions on my brother and sister. They were both minors at the time of these crimes. Do you really think you can prove their culpability after all this time? And make it matter? I don't think so," Gabriel dismissed.

"No. You're right, there probably isn't any way to convict them for something ten years old," Hunter mused. "But your brother is in law enforcement. A few words in the right ear, and his career can take a serious nosedive."

Anger flashed in Gabriel's eyes, telling Danita that Hunter had scored a direct hit.

"Then there's your sister. She does have an actual crime against her." Expressionless, Hunter handed a second file across the desk.

Face hard, Gabriel took it. Danita could almost hear his teeth grinding together as he read the pages.

"As you can see, we have enough to reopen the case against your sister," Hunter pointed out quietly. "Whether we could get a conviction is debatable. But I can't imagine she'd enjoy the trial."

Gabriel looked like he wanted to jump across the desk and beat the hell out of Hunter. Then, like a switch, it all shut off. The fury in his eyes, the air of frustration. Even the tension seemed to flow out of his body. He leaned back and gave Hunter a bored shrug.

"Entrapment and blackmail," Gabriel mused. "You have an interesting game plan here."

"I hear there's a big celebration planned in Black Oak in two weeks," was all Hunter said. But his smile was pure satisfaction. "Hadn't you heard? Your brother is getting married. A Valentine's wedding, as a matter of fact. A week or so of parties, rehearsals, prenuptial fun. I'll bet your family would love for you to be there."

From the shocked look in Gabriel's eyes, he hadn't heard.

And just where did she fit into this little game, Danita wondered. As if reading her mind, Hunter slanted her a look.

"The two of you are going to go to Black Oak under the guise of joining your brother's wedding celebrations," he informed them. "Arrangements have already been made for you to take part in a criminal gathering that's taking place there. Your special skills will appeal to the other guests. You're there to cause discomfort, to gather information and to observe. Not to take any action. After two weeks, your job is done."

"I don't need Blondie for that."

"She'll be there to keep you in line, to solidify your cover and to take over after you've gotten her in the door."

"What cover, and why would I need her?" His gaze was like liquid gold as it slid over her, making Danita feel both hot and just a tiny bit worried at the same time.

"You'll go in as a man who plays the game," Hunter said in a contemplative tone, like a guy weaving a bedtime story. "Your reputation is already established, your talents well-known. So basically, you're going in as yourself. Your goal is to meet a small group of businessmen whose focus is to consolidate power. These are smart men who will quickly see why including you has the potential for multiplying that power. The intel points to an as yet unknown leader who is calling all of the shots. Rumor is that leader is Tobias Black. You know him, his style and his methods well enough to be able to recognize whether that's true or not."

"Screw that," Gabriel growled, tossing the files on the desk. "I'm not going to send up my own father. No way in hell. I'll go to jail myself first."

"Then why don't you take this as a chance to prove his innocence? Before someone else sends him up."

Those words, and the friendly tone of advice that they'd been offered in, made Gabriel pause. He gave Hunter a searching look.

So did Danita. She was baffled. Hunter was usually professional to the point of abruptness. But with this guy, this con artist, he was teetering right over the line into friendliness.

"All you need to do is visit your hometown, be yourself, and listen for information. In and out, no fuss, no muss."

"And Blondie?"

"The men are rumored to be bringing along lady friends for entertainment. Professionals. Danita, basically, is going in as your paid companion."

"My very own hooker," Black said with a taunting smile.

"What?" Forgetting professionalism, to hell with keeping her cool, Danita jumped to her feet. "No! Hunter this was just a fishing trip. You didn't say anything about a long-term assignment."

Not that she'd have said no when he'd brought her on the case. Hunter had been her trainer. He was her boss. Her hero.

And now her pimp?

"This is a bad idea, Hunter. I'm not the right person for this job." Not because she couldn't handle it. Hell, it was right up her alley. But Gabriel Black? Him, she couldn't handle.

She grimaced at the realization.

"I need someone I can trust," Hunter said. "Someone who will use their brain and their instincts while following the rule book. You're my best, Danita. I trust you to handle this job to *my* specifications."

She closed her eyes against that, wishing she could as easily close off the obligation. She didn't know what Hunter was asking of her. Not completely. And she wouldn't unless she accepted the assignment. But she did know, perfectly well, that he was running this case his way, outside the rules. And he was asking her to do the same.

He trusted her.

Which was something very, very few people in her life had ever done.

"What's the primary objective?" she asked quietly.

"To keep Gabriel alive."

That made pretty boy jump. His eyes rounded and he tossed the file on the desk as he shook his head.

"What?" he protested. "Hey now, nobody said anything about risks. I think I'll take my chances with the solicitation entrapment, thank you."

Danita waited for Hunter to shut him down. But her boss only smiled.

"Danita's good. You'll be safe."

"I realize you think you have me over a barrel here, but let's keep it real for a second," Black insisted. "After all, it's apparently *my* life on the line. You have enough to force my hand. But if I play the game, I demand a partner who can handle the job and keep my ass safe."

He gave Danita a long, sexy look. The kind of look that made her breath catch in her throat, her nipples pucker and her mind see red. She hated that look. Hated even more that she was reacting to it. To him. A criminal.

"No offense to the pretty doll here, but other than making one hell of a fake whore, I don't see how she'd be of any help."

The ringing in Danita's ears sounded like a freight train with bells. Her eyes narrowed, her fists clenched. Then she saw that hint of humor in his hypnotic gaze.

He was enjoying this.

The entire process. The arrest, the challenge, the idea of putting his life at risk. It was all a game to him.

And she was playing right into his hands.

All it took was one deep breath to clear the red haze from her eyes, gather her wits and reclaim her poise.

After a quick glance at Hunter for permission, Danita tilted her head to one side and offered Black a chilly smile. "I'm a government agent, Mr. Black."

"So?"

On his face was the same lack of respect Danita usually got from men. Pretty little girls were good for one thing, or for faking one thing. Even here, after four years as an FBI agent, she still saw that look daily.

Frustration was now a bitter, biting ball of fury in her belly. But Danita didn't let him see it. Instead she let her smile slip into condescending.

"So, Mr. Black, not only am I perfectly capable of, how did you put it? Keeping your ass safe? But I'm also the best person for this job. Especially because of my talents as a fake whore, as you so charmingly put it."

Whether she wanted to keep his ass safe was another thing altogether. Danita had to give him credit. From the look on his face, Gabriel Black knew it, too. Maybe he was right to have doubts. She certainly did.

As if sensing her doubts, Hunter handed her a third file. Gabriel frowned, obviously wanting to know what it contained just as much as she did.

Danita flipped it open.

Names of some of the biggest crime bosses in California. A list of the illegal activities suspected of being run from Black Oak. An outline of the extensive criminal web they'd be dealing with. There were notes, not only from Hunter, but from his father. An agent, who, even five years retired, still commanded massive respect. This was a career-making case.

"You in?" Hunter murmured.

She lifted her gaze to his, then shifted her eyes to Gabriel. The man was guaranteed to be a pain in her butt. But the reward if she kept him alive and broke the case?

Incredible. A promotion, yes. But more, a bust that would guarantee her respect among her peers.

The risk?

She was walking into the lion's den without backup. As Hunter's pet project and a favor to his father, this case was off the FBI grid.

"It's your call," Hunter said.

"Hers?" Black protested. "I thought you were in charge of this little game."

"Not any more, Gabriel darling," she purred, "You're going to be taking orders from me now."

IT WAS A WONDER he could breathe, what with the noose looped around his throat. The closer they got to Black Oak, the tighter the ball of anger in his belly got. Gabriel clenched his fists to rein in the frustration.

"I'm the one who knows the area," he snapped to Danita, who was driving a sleek black Corvette like a woman used to commanding powerful beasts. "Why are you the one driving?"

"Because it's my car," she said with a dismissive shrug of one shoulder. "Don't worry. The bad guys won't think you're a wimp for having your girlfriend drive. All you have to do is make a show of playing with your cell phone and claim you were doing some business."

"This is total bullshit," he snapped. Bullshit he'd be ignoring if it wasn't for that damned file. Hunter had a tidy compilation of charges he was ready and willing to level against Gabriel's father in that file. Charges that would humiliate the family, ruin his brother's wedding and break his sister's heart.

"Hunter might believe you can handle this," the blonde said. The quick glance she shot him said she believed nothing of the sort. "But to use your own charming terminology, it's my ass on the front line here. If you can't man up and play the game—and play to win—please, let me know now. I'd rather take a slap on the wrist and a write-up in my file than a bullet over you."

Gabriel rolled his eyes.

"I seriously doubt this situation will involve bullets." And people called him a liar? He was sure this entire thing was a big scam, blown all out of proportion to get him to go along with their little FBI game.

He barely paid attention as she pulled off the highway and motored down a quiet, boringly peaceful road toward the Black Oak Manor. His eyes were locked on Danita, trying to read her.

"We should be safe enough. We're simply gathering information, not pushing any real buttons. Our sources indicate the meeting is being held here at the manor," Danita said as she parked, then killed the engine.

She gave him a veiled glance. "Still, be careful. Word is the stakes are high. Five key crime bosses are here, all with the goal of grabbing the reins of this little alliance. Arrangements have been made to get your name on the guest list, but you're going to have to convince them that you actually have something to bring to the table. Or these guys are likely to toss you out. Or worse."

Bored, Gabriel stared out the window at the manor. A little run-down these days, but mostly it hadn't changed. Given that Black Oak was about two miles up the road, he'd seen the quaint Victorian plenty of times before.

"Are you paying attention?" Danita prodded sharply.

"Babe, the tune is getting old. Your buddy Hunter sang it earlier, now you're humming the same refrain. Big scary criminals are taking over Black Oak. Guns and drugs and the suspicion of money laundering. They're all gathering to hobnob and plan their futures and you're here to crash the party."

"And you still think it's an exaggeration?" she asked, turning in her seat to give him a long look out of those big eyes. Like the night before, those blue eyes were once again smudged and shadowed to make them sultry and huge. Her lips were shiny red this time. And her outfit? Gabriel had damn near swallowed his tongue when she'd let him out of his temporary holding cell that morning—as he'd taken to calling the cheap hotel room Hunter had locked him in.

That glorious body was poured into jeans that showed every dimple, every curve. A tight red cashmere sweater molded over the breasts he'd spent a restless night fantasizing about. Toss in more big curls and a sexy pair of stiletto heels and she was the epitome of a good-time girl with a taste for the expensive.

"Actually, I think it's all bullshit," he said again, trying to focus on the conversation instead of which part of her body he wanted to taste first. "But you've got me by the short hairs so I've got no choice but to play along. So let's go in there, use my connections to get you a room so you can spy on these guys, and clear my debt."

"Just like that? You think you'll just waltz in there, use that charming smile of yours to get a room and then call it done? Like this is nothing?"

"Babe, I'm *sure* this is nothing. If there was an actual problem, I'd have heard. You're claiming my father is being set up to take the fall for some attempted murder, possession of illegal weapons and dealing drugs. I'm saying he's not."

His grin was more wicked than charming as he leaned across the console to rub his thumb over that temptingly plump bottom lip of hers. Even without the shiny gloss, it still looked tasty.

Who knew uptight could be so cute?

Before he could do anything stupid—or stupider, since that mouth was what had got him into this mess in the first place—Gabriel pulled back.

"Let's get this over with," he snapped, losing patience with himself, and with her. He wanted done. If possible, before he had to see anyone in his family.

He'd left this town eight years ago, determined to prove himself. After years of trying to prove himself a worthy partner for his old man, Tobias had chosen someone else. That'd been the last straw for Gabriel. In the ugly, accusation-filled fight on the night of his departure he'd vowed not to have anything to do with his father until he'd proved he was better than the old man by outearning and outconning him. Caleb had called him a stubborn ass. Maya had told him to get over himself. Which had cemented his determination to prove himself.

And now he was back. As a failure. How freaking fabulous. He'd have to find a special way to thank Danita, he mused, giving her a hard look before storming up the walkway.

He didn't know how she kept up with him given that she was wearing those do-me heels, but Danita was around the car and had her hand curled over his before he was halfway up the cobblestone walk toward the manor.

They didn't make it two feet through those wide doors before a goon stopped them. Dressed in an ill-fitting suit, ugly shoes and an uglier expression, the guy hulked inches over Gabriel's six foot two.

"The manor's closed," the guy grunted.

"Where's Ham?" he asked, ignoring him. Instead he addressed the other guy, this one just as ugly but with a better suit. "I'm an old friend with an open invitation to stay here anytime. So why don't one of you boys run out and find him. He owns this place, and he'll vouch for my welcome."

"There's no vacancy right now. Private event this weekend," the taller guy said. With a jerk of his chin, he indicated they get the hell out.

Even though a foot separated them, he could feel Danita tense. She glanced at her fingernails as if inspecting her manicure, then gave him a bored look. But her hand edged toward her purse.

"Ham's an old buddy," Gabriel said, irritated at having to repeat himself. "I'm sure he can squeeze us in."

Before he could blink, the guy by the door shifted. He took two giant steps forward, grabbed Gabriel by the bicep and shifted, pulling his cheap jacket aside. At his waist was a gun. A big, ugly one that looked like it'd make an equally big, ugly hole in someone.

"You were told the manor is closed," the man growled.

Shit.

Every nerve in his body screaming run, Gabriel forced himself to grin as if being threatened with a gun was an everyday occurrence.

That, and a quick glance at Danita assured him that this was some serious shit.

His mind raced, perceptions adjusting at the speed of light. Suddenly this bullshit situation was a high stakes game.

And his father really was in trouble.

Gabriel was a lot of things. A con, a thief and a liar topped the list. But despite the disappointments and problems over the years, he was also a son with an unshakeable love for his father. And he'd be damned if he was going to let a gang of thugs drag his dad down.

"Gentlemen, is this necessary?" he asked with a charming smile that hid his fury. Despite his hatred of all things violent, he reached up and with two fingers, lifted the goon's hand off his own arm.

"I'm Gabriel Black. I'm here for the meeting." He waited a heartbeat, watched the goon and his keeper exchange looks. Then, with a quick, painful thump of his heart, Gabriel committed to the game. Reaching out, he curled his fingers around Danita's wrist and pulled her tight against him.

"My understanding is that we're welcome to bring our own entertainment." Gabriel didn't take his eyes off the taller guy in charge. Ignoring the gun, and Danita's tension, he lifted her hand to his lips. "She's my entertainment."

The guy's eyes slid over Danita with a look so oily, Gabriel was surprised it didn't leave a grease slick.

"She available to entertain anyone else?" the guy asked with a smirk.

A possessive sort of anger that he refused to call jealousy

surged. It was all Gabriel could do to keep from punching the goon in the face.

"For the moment, she's exclusive."

"And later?"

"Son, I don't think you can afford her," Gabriel said with a shrug. "Now if you don't mind, check the guest list or confirm it with Ham, and give me my room key. I've got a few things to do before we get started."

"You got some attitude on you," the goon said, obviously not appreciating being told what to do. The guy was clearly loyal to whoever was in charge.

And just who was that?

Time to get the game going so he could find out.

"Watch it, son" Gabriel warned. "Before this weekend's over, I'm gonna be your boss."

3

DANITA DIDN'T BREATHE easy until the hotel room door closed, leaving the goon who Gabriel had charmed into carrying their bags locked on the other side. She'd been in shoot-outs and hostage situations before, and hadn't broken a sweat.

But getting through the front door of a quaint small town manor, past two gun-toting goons with a cocky guy like Gabriel? Between the cold February air and the sweat soaking through her sweater, she'd be surprised if she didn't catch a darned cold.

As soon as this case was closed, she was telling Hunter that she never, ever wanted to work with a civilian again. Especially not a cocky, criminal one who made her palms sweat and her knees weak.

Although maybe she'd keep that last little bit to herself.

She gave the room a quick glance as Gabriel set their bags next to the dresser. One bed. She knew it was a necessary part of their cover. But, she mentally fanned herself, oh man, this was going to be tricky.

"Well, isn't this the prettiest room I've ever seen? And so expensive, Gabriel. I like expensive," Danita said in a husky tone. She gave him a bland look before adding, "I can't wait to show you just how much I like it."

"You're kidding, right?"

The look he shot her was a combination of irritation and confusion. She held up a finger to silence him before he could put either into words, though. Without much hope, she tapped one finger to her ear to indicate listeners.

Brows drawn together, he gave the room a sweeping glance. He grimaced, then leaned one shoulder against the wall next to the door, rolled his eyes, then said in a natural tone, "Blondie, you prove to me you like it enough and I'll buy you a flashy piece of glitter before the weekend's over."

Clever. Danita kept her face angled to hide her grin. So he wasn't just a pretty-faced liar. He was a smart pretty-faced liar. Who knew?

"What'll it take to get me two bits of glitter?" she asked, her words low and teasing. As she asked, she carefully unzipped the outer lining of her purse to show a clever array of electronic toys. She chose a wand the size of a ballpoint pen, sliding it from its case.

"Maybe the two of us on that bed with a bowl of whipped cream and cherries, followed by a hot-oil tango in the shower," he deadpanned, not shifting from his spot holding up the wall.

The image was so easy to imagine. The two of them, naked on that four-poster bed, rolling over the wedding-ring quilt. Their bodies slick and hot. Desire was like a wave, hitting her hard and fast and damned near sweeping her feet out from under her. Since opening the window to let in cool air would tip him off, she sucked in a discreet breath and forced herself to focus on the job.

And to pretend her hand wasn't shaking.

Like a phone addict looking for cell reception, she ran the tiny wand around the room. It wasn't until she reached the bedside table that the light on the end flashed red. With a warning look at Gabriel, she crouched down and ran her fingers along the side and back of the rich wood. Underneath, she found it. A tiny round bug. She aimed the wand at it and pushed a button. The red light turned green.

Deactivated.

She found two more. One in the phone. And disgustingly, the other in the bathroom just behind the toilet lid. And deactivated both.

She slipped the wand back into its felt case.

Gabriel, still leaning against the wall like he was bored, arched one brow.

She shook her head. She had complete faith that the FBI was a few technological steps ahead of whatever criminals were coming to party this weekend. But it didn't hurt to be careful.

So she pulled out a small device that looked like an MP3 player. Looking around the room, she decided the dresser was about as central as they'd get. She flicked a button on the device. The light glowed white for one second before flashing off. The room filled with a buzzing, then silenced.

"White noise," she said, mentally slapping her hands together as she finished up. "If they have other bugs this'll scramble them. The only way someone's going to hear anything in here is if they are in the next room with a drinking glass against the wall."

"Don't you worry that they're going to be pissed that you broke their toys?"

"I didn't break them. I turned them off." She thought of the welcoming goon squad and shrugged. "They'll be irritated, but probably not surprised. Criminals are notoriously mistrusting."

"You don't say."

Danita turned away, making a show of checking the view out the leaded glass window to hide her smile at his dry rejoinder. Smart, sexy and clever. That added up to an almost irresistible combination.

Before she could decide whether or not to share the smile, though, she saw two new goons patrolling the edge of the forest just beyond the manor's emerald expanse of lawn. Even from this distance, she could see the outline of the submachine guns under their jackets.

She was on the job. Partnered with a criminal. And instead of focusing on the task at hand, she was trying to think of excuses to give in to the hot attraction flaming between them.

It wasn't the same as blowing off her responsibilities for a fifth of Jack and an ounce of weed, but it was too close to that line for Danita's comfort.

What a time for family resemblances to surface. Biting back a furious snarl, Danita pinned her gaze on the largest goon as if she could kick his butt just by glaring. Because her fury was aimed at her own past, and not the man standing behind her, she took a few seconds to get it under control.

Because while she'd happily skewer Gabriel for being a cocky criminal who was crazy-lucky to not be in prison, she wasn't willing to take her own issues out on the guy.

Instead, she took three deep breaths and focused on the reminder that she wasn't her past. Life was about choices, and she'd chosen to close the door on selfish irresponsibility.

And no cleverly sexy criminal was going to make her open it again.

With that in her mind and steel in her spine, she lifted her chin and turned back to the room.

"I can see why you've been such a success as a criminal," she said, her words closed as tight as her expression. "You must be the best liar I've ever watched in action."

"Blondie, that's only the tip of the iceberg. Anytime you want to see what's beneath that tip, you just say the word."

She didn't even bother to sigh. "Men like you just can't

resist pulling out your double entendres to play with, can you?"

"You have no idea what kind of man I am."

"One of a kind, I'm sure," she said in a deliberately bored tone. She was nice enough to turn away before rolling her eyes, though. Needing, desperately, to be busy, she pulled a tiny transmitter and a video camera the size of a safety pin out of yet another cubby in her purse.

"Not quite." Apparently tired of waiting for her to finish her room inspection, he strode over to drop onto the bed. Kicking off his shoes, he spread out, arms crossed behind his head as he rested it on the whitewashed iron headboard.

"I'm a chip off the old block," he said as she surveyed the room. "Not so much in looks, although my brother, sister and I do take after my dad quite a bit. We have our mother's eyes, though. But in personality? Talent? Skill? I'm my old man's son, through and through. But you already know that, don't you?"

Danita paused in the act of running her fingers along the top of the bathroom door frame to stare at him. "You sound like you're proud of that."

"Of course I am."

"Your father is a known criminal. His FBI file is so thick it requires its own drawer. He's rumored to have been involved in scams and cons on five continents, to have had his hand in three major art thefts and to have actually sold some idiot the Golden Gate Bridge." Even though she was the one reciting the list, she still shook her head in wonder. It was hard to believe someone could be suspected of all of that and so much more, yet nobody had ever been able to bust him. *Ever*. She gave Gabriel a baffled look. "And you're proud of your similarities?"

"The man's the best there is. Why wouldn't I be proud?"

Proud. She thought of the door closed tight against her

own past and cringed. Why would either of them want to be aligned with their legacies?

"So why aren't you partnered up with him? Why have you been estranged for the past eight years?"

His eyes narrowed with a frustrated fury that surprised her. Then he blinked and the fury was gone. But Danita wasn't surprised that he changed the subject.

"I'm going to head down to the car," he said. "How long do you think you'll be here playing Jane Bond?"

"Why are you going to the car?" she asked slowly.

"To get the rest of the luggage, of course," he said, slipping his feet back into shoes before giving her a smile that was part charm, part exasperation. "What's the worry? You've got the keys right there, it's not like I can go anywhere."

Eyes narrowed, Danita gave him a long look before nodding slowly. "The head goon said your fellow criminals were all out and about, but just in case, try not to talk to anyone."

"If anyone dares say more than hello, I'll brush them off. You know, tell them I'm in a hurry to get back upstairs for a hot nooner," he tossed over his shoulder with a wicked grin.

With that smile seared in her mind and a gurgle of reluctant laughter lodged in her throat, he was gone.

GABRIEL REVELED IN the power of the Corvette's big block as it tore down the quiet country road.

It was crazy to be disappointed, but he had to admit, he was feeling a little let down. He'd just walked right out of that room, ditching Blondie with hardly any effort at all. You'd think a government-trained agent would be a little smarter. Her car had been in full view of the window, yet she hadn't noticed when he'd boosted it. Or maybe she had and didn't want to blow their cover by chasing him down like an obsessive girlfriend.

He grinned at the image and wondered how long she'd

wait for him to return with the bag before she came looking, then shrugged. Didn't matter. She was pretty enough, and surprisingly not boring. But still, she wasn't his type.

Although he'd love to know how a woman so uptight ended up playing the floozy. And damned if she didn't play an excellent one. Those big blue eyes wide and just a smidge vacant, her lips slick and glossy and that sexy body poured into just enough fabric to make a man sweat. All the while she gave the impression that she was worth every penny in the man's wallet she was grasping.

The memory of her lips under his flashed through his brain like lightning. And through his body like a raging thunderstorm. God, she'd tasted good. Just thinking about her got him hot and hard.

Which was the last thing he needed, he reminded himself as he turned off the highway onto Main and downshifted the 'Vette to something closer to the speed limit.

Ten minutes—and one quick sentimental drive around the town—later he parked his borrowed car in the town square and, one arm across the steering wheel, he looked around with a sigh.

It was the same. A tiny part of him, a part he rarely let see the light of day, relaxed as the warmth of his childhood hometown enveloped him in a welcoming hug.

Damn, he'd forgotten how simply lovely Black Oak was.

Cobblestone walks and brick buildings. Antique lampposts and planter boxes just waiting for the warmth of spring. In the center of the square was a statue of town founder, Gabriel's great-great-grandpa, Andrew Black. Curved iron benches surrounded the square, and in honor of the season, Valentine's hearts decorated the flags waving from various buildings.

A man who rarely allowed sentiment to take hold, he had to smile at the beauty of it all. It was as though he'd never left home.

Before he could get too gooey and emotional, there was a quick rap of knuckles on metal. His gaze flashed to his side-view mirror. A grin, wicked and wide, spread as he swung out of the car.

"Well, well," he said as he leaned one arm on the door-jamb. "What have we here?"

"Trouble, from the look of it," the other man said. Besides an extra inch in height and the really lousy haircut, it was almost like looking in a mirror. That fact had bothered Gabriel growing up.

It was damned hard to stand out within his family. Between his father's rep, his brother's looks and his sister's brains, Gabriel had often wondered what was left for him. Part of why he'd run, he knew. He'd never felt he measured up. Away, he'd been able to find his own strengths, to choose his own priorities.

"You're still sneaking around pretending to be a bad guy?" Gabriel asked, trying to keep the grin from splitting his face at the sight of his brother. God, it'd been close to five years since he'd laid eyes on Caleb, and that'd been a quick, accidental meeting since his brother had been undercover at the time.

"I quit the DEA," Caleb said, leaning his hip against the 'Vette and crossing his arms over his chest and offering one of his long, intense looks.

"And you're back home? The old man finally coaxed you into the fold, huh?"

Caleb's grin was just as wicked as Gabriel's own. With nothing but a slight inclination of his head, he invited his younger brother to look over his shoulder.

Glancing past his brother, it was all Gabriel could do not to cry. He actually felt the tears welling up behind his eyes.

"Say it ain't so," he murmured with a pathetic shake of his head. "You're trying to kill us, aren't you?"

Caleb laughed, following his gaze to look at the sheriff's car parked behind the 'Vette. "Once a rebel."

"Yeah, but at least before you had the decency to rebel elsewhere. Now you've brought it home? You hate Dad that much?"

It'd been bad enough when Caleb had come home right after college graduation to announce that he was joining the DEA.

At least that'd taken him away from California. But now he was back, rubbing his legal activities in Dad's face day in and day out? And they thought Gabriel had issues?

"Dad always said we all have to take our own path," Caleb said with a shrug.

"I don't think he meant for those paths to cut his off at the pass."

"He can take care of himself."

Gabriel considered his brother's face. Caleb had always had a very concrete sense of right and wrong, made all the more obvious since the rest of the family's was so fluid. Given the problems Hunter said were facing their father, which path would Caleb choose? The one that defended family, no matter what the evidence? Or the one that locked the cell door?

"Maybe Dad can take care of himself," Gabriel acknowledged slowly. "But he's got his blind spots. His kids being the main one."

The warning hovered for a long second. Then Caleb gave a shrug, as if batting it away. "You're awfully defensive of a man you haven't bothered to see for yourself in almost a decade," he pointed out.

It was like getting hit in the face with a bagful of guilt. It wasn't as if he'd abandoned his old, decrepit father in a sewer somewhere. Yes, he'd left after an ugly fight, determined to prove himself. Sure, he'd been pissed that Tobias had let some trampy bitch horn her way into the family business. But that wasn't a big deal, dammit. He wasn't ashamed of the vow, or the drama of it. He was irked that he hadn't kept it, though.

"I swore I wouldn't come back until I'd made my point," Gabriel muttered.

"Tough luck, little brother. We all vowed to stay away and we all blew it. Might as well prepare to take Dad's gloating like a man."

"Like you took it?"

"Yep."

Caleb's angry vow had been to never return to Black Oak and look at him now, all spiffed up and in charge of the town's law. Gabriel grinned, feeling a little better. Then the full impact of his brother's words sank in.

"All of us? Maya's here, too?" As he mentally watched the stakes climb higher and higher, the tension returned to Gabriel's shoulders in tight knots. Sure, Hunter had threatened him with trouble for his dad, his brother and sister. But he hadn't realized they were all cozied up together here in Black Oak, easy targets to that trouble.

For Hunter and the FBI.

Or for whatever asshole was trying to ruin Tobias Black.

"Maya's in town for the wedding," his brother stated, the hard line of his jaw softening.

"I can't believe you're really getting married." He didn't quite know what he thought about the prospect of his badass older brother settling down. "And on Valentine's, no less. Isn't wrapping a noose around your neck enough? You have to do it with cupid aiming his arrow at your ass, too?"

Unoffended, Caleb laughed and shrugged. "Pandora's worth it."

"Pandora?" Gabriel prompted.

"Pandora Easton." With a slight inclination of his head, Caleb indicated one of the stores across the street.

Gabriel's gaze cut across the street to the clever display in the window of Moonspun Dreams. It, too, was all decked out for Valentine's, although the hearts in that window were crystal and the signage shouted a sale on love potions. Shocked, he glanced back at his brother for confirmation. "The woo-woo queen's daughter?"

The bar on unbelievable just kept getting higher and higher.

"Yep. That's Pandora. You'll like her," Caleb decreed. "There's a party at the store tonight. Something about welcoming spring or..." He shrugged. "I don't know. Whatever it is, you need to come. You can meet her. See Maya. Deal with Dad."

The twist of Gabriel's lips was more grimace than smile.

"As you yourself pointed out, I haven't seen Dad in a while. With good reason, given that things are pretty ugly between us. I doubt you want to ruin your party with our reunion."

"Pandora's used to bad behavior," was all Caleb said.

Gabriel debated. A part of him, the part that missed his family like crazy, wanted to go. Wanted nothing more than to relax, set the games aside and just be himself for a couple hours. But there was too much at stake.

"We need to talk," his brother said quietly.

Gabriel frowned.

Talk about what? How much did Caleb know about the crime ring playing house at the manor? Did he have a clue that Tobias was being set up for an ugly fall? And how much would he share?

He could push. But his brother used to have the disposition of a granite wall and there was no reason to think that'd changed.

Before he could decide which direction to take, he felt heat.

Like the sun breaking through clouds, warming his back with a tingling awareness.

"There you are, sweetie," a husky voice purred just over Gabriel's shoulder. "I was starting to worry that you'd gone off to have a good ole time without me."

Gabriel's spine turned to steel and he gritted his teeth so hard, he was surprised he didn't bust one.

He hadn't fooled her for one damned second, had he?

Turning slowly, he noted the triumphant look in her big blue eyes, the slight mocking tilt of those glossy lips. And realized that instead of fooling her, he'd played right into her hands.

"I missed you," she said, pressing her body suggestively against his side as she reached up one red-nailed finger to give his chin a chiding tap. She was playing her role to the hilt. "You're a bad boy, running off without me like that."

"Maybe you can spank me later," he suggested dryly.

Amusement broke through her cover for just a second, making her eyes gleam and her lips twitch. But she reeled it in, her eyes taking on that hard edge of a professional. Professional what, he wasn't sure. FBI agent?

He realized she was playing this for Caleb's benefit. But what he wasn't sure of was whether she realized the sheriff she was acting for was yet another of those bad Black boys.

"Did you miss me?" she purred, sliding her hand down his chest with the hint of fingernails. The light scraping, along with the temptation of her touch, put all his senses on full alert. Damn, she was good.

Good enough that Gabriel was having trouble resisting the temptation of her body as it curved into his. She fit perfectly against him, her heels bringing her mouth within kissing distance of his. Her eyes, still tarted up with smudged liner and a heavy coating of mascara, warned him to keep his distance even as her breast warmed his chest.

"You going to introduce your friend?" Caleb prodded, his words just this side of a laugh. Gabriel glanced over to see his brother's eyes glinting with that evil older-brother glee. Maybe he hadn't missed family quite as much as he'd initially thought.

Gabriel gritted his teeth, not sure who he was more annoyed with. Danita for acting all sexy to try and force his hand, pushing him to cement her role as his companion publically. Or Caleb for enjoying this so much.

From the look on Blondie's face, a mix of triumph and absolute confidence that she had his number, she figured she'd won this round.

Which meant she thought he'd lost.

And that wasn't going to happen.

As much to shake her confidence that she was calling the shots as to throw his brother off track, Gabriel pulled Danita against him. Her eyes rounded, tossing all the angry barbs his way he knew she was dying to say but couldn't.

He hadn't planned to go any further. But once her curvy body was hot against his, he couldn't resist. Their eyes locked on each other, Gabriel lowered his mouth to hers. Just a soft brush of the lips. Once, then twice.

If she'd stayed angry—all the way irritated—he'd have let it go at that. But he saw something deeper in those big blue eyes. Heated desire, mixed with just enough curiosity to push all his buttons.

He couldn't resist.

He forgot this was a game of one-upmanship. He forgot she was trying to con his family. He even forgot that his brother was standing there.

All he could think about was Danita. His tongue along the soft cushion of her bottom lip, sipping at the sweet flesh like she was the answer to all his dreams.

The desire in her blue eyes flared.

But she was still playing the game. He could feel it in the way she held her body, the provocative angle that gave the impression that she was curled into him, while in reality she was holding him back. Pushing him away.

He slid one finger along her jaw, down the sweet softness of her throat. And took pleasure in the shudder she couldn't hold back.

Needing more, needing desperately to push her for more, he took the kiss deeper. His mouth slid along hers, coaxing and tempting. After a brief hesitation, her lips softened, her tongue tangled.

Drowning, was all Gabriel could think. He was drowning in her. That thought terrified him. Slowly, reluctantly, he pulled back. And watched her blue eyes blink the passion away in one sweep of those thick lashes.

In an instant, she went from hot to cold. From passionate to calculating.

God, what a woman.

Unable to stop his grin from spreading, Gabriel wrapped one arm around her shoulder to keep her close and turned so they faced his brother.

Caleb was watching, one brow arched and a look of amused patience on his face. Gabriel knew what Danita expected of him. He thought of that clever FBI trap Hunter had outlined. He had a pretty good idea of what his family was up to and just what they were risking here.

He quickly calculated the risk of running a con with the odds this high. With so much at risk.

Then, Blondie's body warm and soft against his side, he figured what the hell.

"This is Danita," Gabriel introduced. "She's my fiancée."

4

"WHAT THE HELL WERE you thinking?" Danita ranted, pacing the frustratingly short space between the window and the bathroom.

She'd been bitching the same tune for the past half hour. Ever since they left his brother in town. A brother who had a gorgeous smile, a body to rival Gabriel's for hunky-man-of-the-month, and a look of suspicion so strong in his eyes, she was surprised he hadn't tried to fingerprint her then and there.

But so far, none of her bitching had resulted in anything other than a shrug out of Gabriel.

"I'm serious," she insisted. "Why would you tell your brother something like that? Do you not care what's at stake here?"

She didn't know if her voice had finally wore him down or if Gabriel had just finished whatever it was that he'd been concentrating on while staring out the window. Either way, something made him turn to face her. One shoulder leaning against the window frame, he gave her a long, bored look.

"What?" he asked. "I was supposed to introduce you to my brother as my hooker? A high-end call girl with a taste for crime?"

Even in her anger, she had to appreciate that he didn't toss in the third option—to out her as an FBI agent there to break a crime ring. After all, they didn't know for sure who might be listening. And while Hunter's files cleared Caleb Black, they didn't indicate whether he would support the FBI or whether he'd side with his father.

"You were supposed to stick with the relationship we agreed to," she snapped. "We're here to gather information, not to weave a wider web of lies."

"That might work for here," he said waving his hand around the room to indicate, she supposed, the entire manor and the cover they'd agreed to use for the meetings. "But it wouldn't work in town and it won't work for my family."

"Why? Because they expect you to be cozily settling into domestic bliss with me?"

God, why did that image terrify and exhilarate her in equal parts?

"No. But they don't expect, and won't accept, the inclusion of a cheap—or in your case, Blondie, expensive—bimbo at any family events. And since I'm here to clear my father, I'll be attending a great many family events. Were you planning to wait here in the room?"

Danita hissed, as much over his description, accurate though it was, as for his insight. And his thoughtfulness. He hadn't hid his feelings. He hadn't wanted her here, nor had he wanted any part of the case itself. Hunter had blackmailed him, using that family Gabriel was so hot to protect as a lever.

But he was taking steps to make sure she was included. Not only tolerated, but welcomed to whatever family gathering he might attend.

Even though she knew he hadn't done it to make her life easier, or to help with the case, it was still a nice thing to do. It'd make things easier on his family, and on her.

"It could ruin our cover here," she said quietly, not letting go of her frown completely. Just because he did something thoughtful didn't mean she was letting him call the shots on this case.

"Nah. Not when my esteemed colleagues here find out I'm lying about you in order to set my old man up. They think I'm here to screw him over and I'll be a shoo-in as president of their West Coast criminals club."

Had she considered him thoughtful?

Horrified, she had to drag her jaw shut.

"You'd do that? Use your family to con these criminals?"

"You are," he pointed out.

Danita wanted to protest. She was doing her job. She was trying to break a crime ring and maybe, just maybe, catch a notorious con artist.

That the notorious con was Gabriel's father was beside the point. She wasn't trying to use him. Just to arrest him.

Before she could decide how to respond to Gabriel—before she could even figure out what she felt about it—there was a knock on the door. Training chilled her eyes and calmed her mind. Confusion cleared, worry disappeared.

This would be contact.

This was why she was here.

Giving Gabriel a warning look, she gave her reflection a quick glance in the mirror. A second to fluff her hair, another to slide one ankle against the other as a reminder that her gun was readily available, and she was ready.

She arched another warning look at Gabriel, then tugged the door open with a sultry smile.

"H'lo," she murmured.

"Meeting time," the goon said, ignoring her to look across the room at Gabriel. "Ten minutes. Dining room."

"We'll be there."

Danita held her breath, watching the goon's frown crease his wide face. She and Hunter had suggested Gabriel try to bring her to the meetings, but they knew the probability he could pull it off was slim. She'd planned for him to wear a wire, at least until she had a chance to bug the meeting room.

"Not we. Just you."

Gabriel shifted away from the wall, straightening to his full height. It was like watching a warrior pull on armor. He became dangerous. Intimidating. Danita licked her lips. And so damned tempting.

"We. She's a part of my plan."

"You're not here to pitch your plan. You're here to listen."

"I have inside connections and pull that none of you could even dream of." Gabriel's words were so strong, so assured, that Danita wondered just what he had up his sleeve. "Your little club needs me. So we do things my way. Or I leave."

It was like watching an ocean liner try to turn on a dime. The guy's brain was just too slow to keep up, and wasn't programmed for options other than relaying orders.

"Your neck," the goon finally said with a shrug. Then he glanced at his watch and said, "Nine minutes."

Danita closed the door on his retreating back. She took a deep breath, suddenly worried about Gabriel's safety. Only because he was basically in her custody, she assured herself. Not because she actually cared about the guy.

"What are you planning?" she asked.

"I told you, I'm going to con them all. Make them think I have the inside info to set up my old man. If that's really their goal, they'll snap me up. If they want more, I have a few other ideas to play with, too," he said as he shrugged out of his leather jacket and hung it up.

She wanted to ask what ideas. She needed to know what he was planning.

But then his fingers went to the buttons of his shirt.

Her heart skipped a beat.

Each button revealed more skin. Gorgeous, silky golden

skin covered with a light dusting of black hair. Her mouth watered. Then he pulled off the shirt and she swore she felt the room spin a couple times. Gorgeous. Subtle muscles made his broad shoulders and well-toned chest a work of art. His biceps flexed as he bunched the shirt up and tossed it in the laundry bag hanging in the closet before flicking open his suitcase to pull out a fresh black shirt. A quick shake of the fabric to release wrinkles made the muscles of his back dance in the mirror.

She wanted, desperately, to run her tongue over that skin and taste him in tiny, nibbling bites.

"What are you doing?" She hated that her words were breathless, but her mouth was too busy trying not to let the drool slide down her chin to worry about sucking in air.

"Getting ready for the meeting. Appearances are everything, Blondie. You should know that." He slanted her an amused look that made it clear he knew how he was affecting her. Then, as he pulled his shirt on and strode toward the bathroom, he arched one brow.

"You might want to spiffy it up a little. Sexy casual is good, but we're going in there to take control. We want to control the scene, call the shots. These guys are all about intimidation. So we need to go in there playing rich and powerful, making it clear they'd be lucky to have us in their club. They're the ones who end up intimidated."

"By dressing *spiffy?*" she asked.

"Sexy casual," he said, tossing her a grin. "But rich. I'm a wealthy man, remember."

With that and a wink, he closed the bathroom door on his huge ego and gorgeous shoulders.

Danita ground her teeth together. She was the agent in charge, and he was telling her how to dress her part?

Well, that dried up the drool all right. Easily ignoring the memory-tempting golden sheen of all those hard muscles,

Danita tossed her suitcase open. Mostly she'd packed upscale hooker clothes. But upscale sexy was easy enough to pull together. She just combined her own taste with her undercover look.

She pulled out a black leather pencil skirt, and to keep the slit up the back from edging into slutty, she added black opaque tights and a pair of patent leather pumps. After a brief consideration, she pulled out a severe white button-up shirt in one hand, and a tight black cashmere sweater in the other, debating both looks.

"Go for the sweater," Gabriel said as he stepped out of the bathroom. "It's sexier."

Sweater in hand, she turned to gather the rest of her outfit before glancing at him.

Why was the man so heart-stoppingly gorgeous? He'd skipped the tie, taking his suit down from formal to simply powerful. The black fabric looked rich, making her fingers tingle with the need to touch it, to slide her hands over his shoulders to see if it was as luxurious feeling as it looked. His black shirt was open at the collar, showing off just enough skin to keep the image of him, shirtless, firmly in her mind.

"Better hurry," he said. "We're gonna be late."

Better hurry because she was going crazy, she told herself as she rushed to the bathroom. He was key to breaking this case, she reminded herself. He was under her protection. They were undercover. In less than ten minutes, they would be facing a roomful of the top criminals on the West Coast.

As she slicked on a pale pink gloss over her lips and fluffed her hair, Danita realized that none of that mattered. Not compared to those gorgeous shoulders.

What mattered, dammit, was that he was a con artist with a reputation for having almost as many crimes as his father.

Thirty minutes later, as Danita settled in a plush easy

chair in a corner of the manor's private dining room, she was forced to adjust her opinion.

Gabriel Black wasn't just a con. He was the best damned con artist she'd ever met.

Six guys flanked the long oak table, many of whom Danita recognized from their FBI files. Three of them had personal goons standing at attention behind their chairs. The others didn't rate goons, but had their jackets pulled open to show off their holstered hardware.

And then there was Gabriel.

Unlike the other guys, he wasn't flexing any muscle. He'd brought her, his pseudo-girlfriend, instead of a hired goon. They'd waltzed in here late, and from the second he'd stepped through those pretty stained glass doors, he'd been in charge. Despite the murmured protests that it was saved for someone—just in case—he'd commandeered the seat at the head of the table.

After introducing himself and getting the names of everyone in the room, goons included, he'd taken the lead in the discussion. There were a few angry looks, some mutters and grumbles, but nobody stopped him.

It was like watching a master conductor lead a symphony, he was playing them so well.

"I'm impressed with the experience and credentials everyone is bringing to the table here," Gabriel said comfortably after one of the guys she didn't recognize had passed around drinks. Danita made a mental note to find out who he was. Gabriel clearly knew, even though the guy hadn't participated in the introductions.

"Our résumés aren't any of your business," the man to Gabriel's left said. "We here to discuss forming a West Coast coalition. Not voting for class president."

"All ventures, including a coalition, require a leader," Gabriel said easily.

"And you think you're the man for the job," a huge man grumbled at the end of the table. Danita recognized him as Larson Yarnell, a known gunrunner.

"I think we all bring special skills to the table," Gabriel said easily. "I wouldn't try to tell you the ins and outs of smuggling weapons, Yarnell. Just like I have complete trust in Adams's skills with internet fraud. Throw in Mikels's drug connections, Banding's theft rings and the rest of the connections in this room as we've got the makings of a solid coalition."

From the shocked looks around the table, the men clearly hadn't expected Gabriel to know that much about who they all were and what they did.

"What're you bringing to the table?" Mikels asked quietly, a beam of light shining through the window to gleam off his bald head.

"Me? I bring a talent for organization to the table. I'm a man who knows how to make things happen. How to put all the elements together, arrange them in a way that makes the most money and benefits."

"So?"

"So, I have the skill to bring all of your talents together in a way that will make us all very, very rich." Gabriel's smile flashed pure charm, but didn't seem to be affecting the men around the table. Danita wondered if they'd overestimated talent. Maybe Hunter had called this wrong.

"We're already rich, and this deal is guaranteed to get us a whole lot richer. Why would we need you?"

"Guaranteed?" Gabriel's skeptical smile elicited more than one growl around the table.

"We follow the boss's plan and pool our resources. Instead of all of us controlling bits and pieces of illegal activities, together we can control the entire state. Eventually, the country."

"Clever." Gabriel's nod acknowledged the plan, but doubt was written all over his face. What was he up to? "It sounds to me like someone's thought it all through very carefully. Brought you all together to contribute your piece of the pie, right?"

"And just what's your piece?" Mikels asked, his mud-brown gaze sliding over Danita like a slug.

Gabriel shifted, just a couple of inches. The move made him seem bigger. More intimidating. The air in the room changed. Chilled. A couple of the goons shifted nervously.

"Mind your manners," Gabriel murmured with a pleasant smile that offered the same lethal threat as an AK-47. Without blinking, he waited for the other man to shrink into his chair before telling the table, "What I offer, gentlemen, is a skill for playing the game. I'm best at assessing the situation and calling the shots. Which is why I was invited, right?"

A few of the men shared frowns and muttered glances. Jealousy? Or were they wondering just how, exactly, Gabriel had got himself added to the guest list. Tension knotted in her stomach, Danita carefully watched the men for sudden moves. After all, Gabriel's invitation had been the work of the FBI and a hacker unknown to her. What if one of these guys knew the real guest list?

"It's up to the boss," a man said from his position by the door at the opposite end of the room. The guy who'd passed around drinks. Apparently he was the host of their little party. Danita frowned. He didn't have the build of a thug, but wasn't on any of the FBI's wanted lists either.

"Boss, Ham?" Gabriel asked. Ham? Hamilton Bollinger, Danita realized. The owner of the manor, a local business-man, as Danita recalled, who had a relatively clean record.

Clearly his record was missing some vital information.

Gabriel met the older man's gaze as he leaned back in the chair, looking completely relaxed. "And just who is this boss,

Ham? Why isn't he here to run this little show himself? Too busy, right? Which is why he needs me."

Adams laughed, a mean sort of sound that usually preceded a gut kick or knife in the back. "You don't think we'll let you waltz in here and claim top spot, do you, pretty boy?"

"Let me?" Gabriel asked. His words were quiet. His expression friendly. But the air in the room sizzled with a potential for violence that had Danita calculating how long it'd take her to grab the pistol strapped to her inner thigh.

"Enough," the guy Gabriel had called Ham barked. "The boss is calling the shots and will continue calling the shots. This week's meetings are to solidify the West Coast plans, and to figure out who will be the front man."

"You still haven't told us why this guy couldn't be bothered to be here for the meeting," Gabriel challenged, making a show of looking around the room. "We're here. We all bring something to the table. And we're supposed to, what? Align our skills and resources to someone who doesn't even bother to show up? Someone we don't know?"

And just like that, the energy shifted again. Suddenly the glares were aimed at Ham, with the men clearly stepping over to Gabriel's team.

"I don't know about the rest of you, but I don't work blind. While I can see the benefits of this coalition idea, I don't need it," Gabriel said with a shake of his head. "If I'm going to play, I want to see the team. The entire team."

"You're not calling the shots," Ham said, wiping sweat off his forehead with a trembling hand. "You don't get to make demands."

"What I am is the man with the key," Gabriel said with a charming smile. He waved his hand—no trembles in sight—around the table. "Unlike the rest of these fine gentlemen, I'm not looking for a new connection or a chance to sell my wares to a bigger audience. I'm here for one reason."

"What's that?" Ham asked, his previously nervous demeanor suddenly shrewd.

"Revenge."

That caused a few mutters, but mostly garnered him approving looks. These guys were all about the revenge concept.

"Against?" Ham prodded.

"My father, of course. Your boss has already built the frame, setting him up for that drug deal last month, the guns a few weeks ago. It wasn't a bad job. Not bad at all." Gabriel flashed a wicked smile. "But I can do better. Your boss has a reason for setting Tobias Black up. I'm the key to making that setup solid, and making it work."

Her heart pounding, Danita held her breath. None of her worry or anger showed on her face. But she was still freaked out.

They didn't know for sure that Tobias Black wasn't the one behind this plan. Sure, Gabriel was hoping he wasn't. But what if he was wrong? Ham was taking direct orders from someone, and if that someone was Tobias, their cover was blown.

If it weren't for the room filled with people who'd be happy to kill them, Danita would jump up and smack Gabriel. What the hell was he doing? They were here to get information. Not to play games. They wanted the name at the top. She'd carefully outlined what was and wasn't acceptable in eliciting that information during their drive up. And he, of course, was ignoring every damned order she'd made.

But nobody said a word. Trying to gauge the reactions, she heaved a sigh, as if bored silly, and inspected her manicure while scanning the men around the table from the corner of her eye. He was making it work. The criminals looked intrigued, a few were impressed that he'd so happily sell out his own father.

And Ham, the guy with the direct line to the person behind all of this and the key to it all? He was practically bouncing in his boots with excitement.

Damn Gabriel Black for being scary good at this game.

"Tell you what, you share that little bit of news with your boss. Then you get back to me." Gabriel stood, his smile confident and cold. "I've got the talent to lead this coalition. And I've got the connections to pull off the con. But I won't use either until I meet, face-to-face, with the person calling the shots. If I'm in, I'm in charge. You gentlemen won't mind, right?"

Busy scanning the faces and filing away reactions, Danita almost missed the hand Gabriel held out to her.

"C'mon, Blondie. Let's give these gentlemen time to decide whether to ante up or fold."

Her fingers trembled just the tiniest bit in Gabriel's hand as she followed him from the room. His fingers tightened, warming the worry from hers.

As soon as they reached the top of the stairs and the hallway leading to their room, he grabbed her shoulders and swung her against the wall. His body pressing tight against hers, Gabriel's grin was gleefully wicked.

"Babe, that was fun. Nothing like the rush of playing a major con."

"You're crazy," she breathed. Then, swallowing a relieved giggle, she gave in to that rush by linking her fingers behind his neck and grinning up at him. "And baby, you played that room like a virtuoso."

"Encore time," he said as his lips met hers. That same edgy danger that she'd felt in the room was here on his lips as they took hers. Nipping, pushing, demanding. His kiss said he knew what she had and he wanted it all. Her body, just moments ago tight with nerves, melted into a puddle of lust, held up only by the pressure of his and the wall behind her.

But when his hand slid up her hip, under the cloud-soft fabric of her sweater to touch her bare skin, it was like he'd pinched her awake from a very sexy dream.

"No," she murmured, pulling her mouth from his. "We can't."

"Blondie, we definitely can." His body pressed a little tighter against hers, the hard length of his erection echoing his promise.

"No." Horrified at how hard it was—saying no, not the erection—she pressed both palms against his chest to put some space between them so she could slide under his arm.

She was on the job. He was a criminal, a man who in any other situation she'd be trying to arrest.

Danita didn't look back. As fast as she could in her platform pumps, she hurried up the wide sweep of stairs. She needed distance. She needed to think.

Most of all, she needed control.

Never before had she been so turned on. Not by a kiss, not by a man. And definitely not by watching a criminal pull strings and play a room full of dirtbags.

Shoving the door to their room open, she let it slam against the wall as her eyes blurred with tears. Gasping for breath, she hurried to the bathroom where she locked the door—a feeble barrier—and splashed cold water on her cheeks until she regained control.

"You've worked your ass off for this career," she told herself, glaring a warning at her reflection. "You've spent the last ten years escaping the prison of that damned trailer park life. You will not, dammit, blow it over one sexy man."

She took a deep breath, noting the desire-dilated pupils and flush coating her from cleavage to hairline. Her nipples were sharp points through the soft black fabric of her sweater.

"No matter how sexy he is. Despite the fact that you've

never felt anything like this, ever before, it's not worth blowing your life over."

Her lecture warring with the montage of images of Gabriel—his bare skin, his wicked grin and the cleverly cocky way he'd manipulated the situation.

Danita closed her eyes and tried to call up the image of her childhood home, that broken-down trailer, the guttural sounds of yet another of her mother's drunken hookups coming from the front room while Danita was locked in the back.

That's what falling for a pretty face and clever line brought the women in her family. That, and a broken heart. The lure of sex had proven, over and over again, to be kryptonite for her mother, her aunt, even her grandmother.

Danita's job, embracing her career, had got her away from that life. Through it, she'd proven she wasn't like her family.

So do your job, she thought as she stared at herself in the mirror. *Do the job, and watch your ass.*

5

GABRIEL STOOD IN the town square, in the exact same spot he had reunited with his brother earlier. As the cool night air washed over him, he glared across the street at the brightly lit New Age store.

He'd once conned a dinner party of twenty crooked business executives, convincing them to invest in a movie he'd claimed was in production. He'd named actors, locations, everything. The chances of that con blowing up in his face had been huge. The risk of conning a bunch of thieves had been major.

And he hadn't been nearly as nervous then as he was now, preparing to face his family.

"Are you going to be able to pull this off?" Danita asked behind him. Her tone was matter-of-fact. Abrupt, even. But he heard the concern, and just a little bit of sympathy, beneath her words. He wished she wasn't with him. It was bad enough being forced back into the family fold. But doing it with an FBI escort really chafed.

Since that FBI escort was the sexiest thing he'd ever tasted—a flavor he was worried he could become addicted to—the part that was chafing was pressed against his zipper.

Gabriel glanced over at Danita, noting that she'd toned

down her look for the party. Instead of teased and poofed, her hair was sleek and soft around that pretty face. Her makeup was low-key. Not as severe as she'd looked in Hunter's office as FBI Barbie, not as over-the-top as she looked as a hooker-on-the-prowl. This Danita was somewhere in between. This Danita, he suspected, was much closer to the real her.

The real her had the power to drive him crazy. Sexy with just enough sweet to tug at his emotions. Clever with just enough edge to keep him on his toes.

He could pull this con off. He knew he could, even though the layers of it, the multi-cons within cons, would be the biggest scam he'd ever played.

But the game with Blondie?

That one he could very well lose.

"Look, maybe we should—"

"Maybe we should get inside before we freeze out here," Danita interrupted. She reached out as if to tug him along, then, before she made contact, she pulled her hands back and stuffed them in the pockets of her heavy wool pea coat.

"Eager to arrest my father?" he asked, surprised at the bitter undertone to his words.

"Aren't you the one setting up your family?" she said with a knowing look.

Only for their own good, he wanted to say. He was here to protect them and to prove his father's innocence. Or, if his deepest fear was realized and his father really was behind all of this, to deflect the con and make him look innocent. So if that meant setting them up, so be it.

Still, Gabriel frowned before he realized that it wasn't judgment in her big blue eyes. It was understanding. He didn't want her to understand, though. That made her way too appealing. Frustrated on levels he hadn't even realized he had, Gabriel gave a bad tempered shrug.

"I don't like this," he confessed.

She arched one brow and tilted her head in question. He wanted to ignore the silent request. But she had a way of making him want to share. To trust her.

Knowing trust was the first step to ruin, Gabriel shoved one hand through his hair and turned his frustrated gaze back on the store. He could see people milling about through the window, laughing and having a good time. He didn't belong there. He had no business bringing this ugly game into that happy place. "It's hard, okay?"

"It, what?" she asked, her soft tone barely carrying over the cold February night air.

"It, coming home. It, facing my family. It, playing this game." He met her eyes, not sure if he was happy or more frustrated to see the understanding in those pretty blue depths. "It, bringing you here to meet them, knowing you're judging them. Judging me."

Her eyes softened, making him feel like an idiot. Gabriel didn't know what the hell was going on, but he didn't like it. He never felt nervous. And he never admitted this kind of stuff. Clearly because it made him feel stupid.

"Look, forget I said anything," he told her. His gaze cut back to the store again, the warm light shining through the windows an invitation he wasn't sure he wanted to accept any longer. "Let's forget all of this. We'll go somewhere. Get dinner."

"Avoid the issue?"

"Sure," he said, dredging up a bittersweet smile that was probably a little too short on charm. "Emotional avoidance is one of the keys to a good con."

"And a good undercover case," Danita said, her own smile fading a little. He wondered if it was because she'd just realized they had a little more in common than she'd thought. Whatever the reason, her gaze turned serious and she gave him a long look that said the bullshitting was over. "I have a job to do. Which means following through on this invitation tonight. I'm sure we'll get more information at this party than we would sitting in our hotel room. There's a lot at stake, Gabriel. Including the people you care about."

He didn't give a damn about her case. But he did care, way too much, about the people in that store.

And about protecting them.

Which, after the meeting this afternoon with the goon squad, was going to be very necessary. Because he was sure the bad guys' main goal was to take down Tobias Black.

So he had to go in. He had to gather as much information as he could to figure out what game was being played. Once he saw the players, gauged the rules, he could start eliminating until he'd found the kingpin behind it all. And he had to do it with his hottie FBI girlfriend by his side.

Damn it.

They crossed the street. At the door of Moonspun Dreams Gabriel met Danita's eyes and saw both preparation and assurance. Reaching out, he grabbed the brass handle and pulled open the heavy door.

And came face-to-face with Maya.

Gabriel was steeled, emotionally. Hell, he'd faced down a roomful of armed crooks just a few hours ago.

Seeing family should be nothing.

Except when it was his little sister's face.

Maya grinned. Her eyes, the same gold as his, flashed with joy. Then, just enough warning for him to brace himself, she launched herself into his arms with a loud whoop.

"You're here. Here, here, here. I can't believe how much I missed you." Maya pressed a kiss on his left cheek, another on his right, then a smacking loud one right on the lips. "You look fabulous."

Happiness filled Gabriel as he hugged her tight. God, he'd missed her too. Setting her back a foot, he looked his fill. His little sister was all grown up. The sweet-cheeked baby fat she'd sported at eighteen was gone. Black curls waved to her waist over a red sweater. Her smile was the same, though.

"You look great," he told her. Giving in to a need he hadn't realized he had, he rested his forehead against hers and breathed deep her flowery scent. "I missed you, brat."

For one single second, Gabriel wanted to come clean. To blow off the con—all of the cons—and make things right with his family. Straight-up right, with no games.

Then he blinked and the urge was gone. Because he couldn't make things right without people getting hurt. In a twisted way, it was his responsibility to con those he loved. For their own good, of course.

"I'm so glad you're here," Maya said, stepping back but not letting go of his hand. She looked past his shoulder, widening her smile. "And you brought a friend."

A friend. It took Gabriel a few seconds to realize the feeling he had as he turned to face Danita was guilt. Shrugging it off, he reached out his free hand to take Danita's and pull her closer.

"Maya, I want you to meet Danita." He glanced at his FBI keeper, his warning look turning to confusion when he saw the soft understanding in her pretty blue eyes. She was killing him with her sweetness. The stomach-clenching sexual awareness, he could handle.

"Hi Danita," Maya was saying. "It's lovely to see you. Come on in, meet the rest of the family."

Gabriel let his sister pull him, and in turn Danita, through the store. It was like a quick trip through a different world. He'd never seen anything like Moonspun Dreams. Crystals and candles, tarot cards and jewelry, goddess statues and bundles of herbs. And then there were the customers. Women in feathers, men in tunics, the scent of incense mingling with lavender as the exotic and eccentric noshed on appetizers and laughed over drinks.

He held Danita's fingers tight so she didn't get lost in the weirdness. It had nothing to do with the sudden need to keep her close. It was for her own protection, since some of these people, especially the guy with the solar system tattooed on his forehead, looked a little dangerous.

As skilled as he was at lying, even he didn't believe that crap. But he didn't let go of her hand.

"Why are we here again?" he muttered.

Maya shot a laughing grin over her shoulder. "Isn't this great? A whole busload of people show up here a few times a year, looking for spiritual nirvana and a good time. And, of course, a reading by Cassiopeia."

They reached the sales counter. A long expanse of carved rosewood, it seemed to be the border between New Age nirvana and the promise of some semblance of normalcy.

"I'm impressed by how big the crowd is," Danita said, offering Maya a friendly smile. "I had no idea a... What did you call it, Gabriel? A celebration of the return of spring?"

"That's what Caleb said." Gabriel shrugged. Early February seemed like a crazy time to celebrate spring, but what did he know.

"Imbolc is a big holiday in Pandora's family. Moonspun Dreams goes all out to celebrate, but usually it's just their clientele," Maya explained. "But this year, Aunt Cynthia talked Cassiopeia into making it a bigger event. You know, bring in the locals. She figured it was a good time to stir up support for her bid for state representative."

Gabriel looked around, noting that among the more esoteric guests, the party was sprinkled with people he recognized. His high school shop teacher, a few old neighbors. An ex or two and a number of others he remembered from growing up here. And this was the crowd his aunt was trying to mooch political money from? His shoulders tensed.

There were even a few gentlemen from the manor here. Were they up to something? A meeting, perhaps? Or instructions? Gabriel made a note to keep an eye on Ham and just who he chatted with. His fingers tightened on Danita's. She gave him a questioning look. He tilted his head. She glanced around, then met his eyes with a wide-eyed frown.

"It's a great crowd, huh?" Maya asked, stopping at the counter to gesture to the array of drinks set out. Gabriel took a bottle of water for himself and for Danita, figuring neither of them needed alcohol for this event. He continued to scan the crowd, his gaze now sweeping the people gathered in the café.

"Aunt Cynthia really thinks she's going to get political support from this crowd?" Gabriel asked, slightly awed at the idea that their austere and uptight mayor would attend this kind of party.

"Yep. She's talking herself up to everyone here. I don't think her run for congress is going too well. You know how it is, grassroot funds versus big-city donor pools." Maya gave a rueful shrug. She'd always been closer with their aunt than her brothers, which meant she had a much higher tolerance. Gabriel? He'd just as soon avoid her as he would the goons on the other side of the room.

"C'mon," Maya said, gesturing them back toward the café. "Caleb's hiding in the back, but I know he wants you to meet Pandora. I saw her sneak into the kitchen a few minutes ago to replenish the aphrodisiac appetizers."

Gabriel shared a baffled look with Danita, wondering what the hell had happened to Black Oak. They didn't need an FBI investigation. More like a psychiatric evaluation.

Mulling the changes and trying to adjust his memory of a confining small town with the idea that his future sister-in-law was whipping up sex food, he made it two steps past the counter and stopped short. Unprepared, Danita ran into him, her breasts crushed against his arm as she looked around to see why he'd stopped. Sexual awareness sparked, even as his stomach clenched.

"Son."

A million thoughts, untold emotions slammed through Gabriel. He could see judgment mingled with the love and pride in his father's gaze. A sense of failure, one Gabriel always felt at not being better, smarter, quicker than everyone else, trickled in like cold snow down the back of his neck. Would he ever measure up? He wasn't as good as Caleb. He wasn't as clever as Maya. Would he ever feel like a success in his father's eyes?

"Dad," he greeted quietly.

"Welcome home." For a brief second, Tobias looked like he was going to step forward and offer an embrace. Gabriel didn't know if he was grateful or disappointed when his dad offered a nod instead. "It's good of you to make time for your brother's wedding."

Fighting off feelings of disappointment and emptiness that his father had held back, Gabriel told himself it was just as well. A big ole hug from Dad wouldn't do much to cement his role in town, and he could see the goons watching closely.

"Wouldn't miss it. Seeing big brother married off, that's worth the price of admission." Happy to have a direction, Gabriel's gaze cut to Caleb who'd come up behind their father.

"Gabriel, this is my fiancée," Caleb said. Tobias stepped aside so Gabriel could clearly see the woman next to his brother. She reminded Gabriel of an angel, with her creamy complexion, smooth fall of auburn hair and sweet expression. "Pandora, this is my little brother, Gabriel."

"Little?" Pandora said with an easy laugh as she stepped over to shock Gabriel with a warm hug. "It's wonderful to meet you. I've heard so many things and now you can tell me which are true and which are your brother and sister trying to get you in trouble. Come back, I've saved us a table."

Gabriel hesitated. There was a show to put on here and he knew the success of his con depended on his audience's belief in the part he played as the angry son.

But he couldn't. Just couldn't push the confrontation with Tobias. Not here, in front of all these people. Not now, when he was still reeling from the emotions of seeing his family again.

He'd spent so many hours over the last eight years imagining what he'd say the first time he saw his father again. The words he'd use to pound his success home. But now, instead of throwing his accomplishments in his father's face, he gave his dad a nod. Then, his hand still wrapped around Danita's, he followed the pretty redhead through the café to a small table by the kitchen.

"I've got to admit, any stories they've shared about me and trouble are probably true," Gabriel said with a quick smile as Caleb pulled out a chair for his fiancée.

Finally letting go of Danita, and feeling oddly bereft, Gabriel did the same, waiting until she'd sat before taking his own seat. He glanced quickly around, noting that instead of joining them, Tobias was seated across the room chatting with Maya, a look of supreme satisfaction on his face.

What he had to be so smug and happy about, Gabriel didn't have a clue. Usually that look was saved for gloating after a con was done. Gabriel wondered if he'd wear that same look on his face when he left town next week. His stomach clenched tight for just a second as he realized that if he did, it would be because he'd pulled a major con on everyone in this room. A con that would cost him his relationship with all of them. As long as it meant exonerating his father, he'd have to be satisfied. It wasn't like he was losing anything he hadn't already given up.

"Gabriel?" Pandora said quietly, pressing her fingers lightly to the back of his hand. "Are you okay?"

"Yeah. I'm okay," he lied. He'd have to be. A man didn't take the risks he did without being willing to pay the price. "I'm just enjoying this little family reunion."

And wondering at the vicious timing of fate, that he now realized for the first time in his life just how much he wanted, needed, his family. And that by this time next week, he would, quite likely, have ruined any chance of reconciling with any of them.

He glanced at the pretty blonde sitting next to him, her eyes sharp as she looked around the room like she was taking a criminal inventory.

Just doing her job, he realized. A part of him wanted to hate her for dragging him back here. For making him face what he'd lost, and accept that to save his family he had to give them up.

The rest of him, though, was still remembering how she'd tasted. What her body had felt like pressed against his. And wondering just how long it'd take to taste her—to feel her—again.

DANITA WAS MISERABLE.

Her stomach hurt. Not from the appetizers a roving waiter had brought around, which had been delicious. But from guilt.

Her head ached. Not from the conversation, which was entertaining and fun, but from stress.

These people were not what she expected.

Instead of a family of hardened criminals and weak-willed sycophants, they were all nice and friendly. Laughter and teasing, great food and warm conversation.

Between chatting to any partygoers who stopped at their table to visit, Caleb doted on Pandora. He'd listened to his sister's teasing about wearing a top hat and tails for the ceremony with an easy grin. Maya was like a cheerful ray of sunshine, beaming at everyone like a kid on Christmas morning. She went from conversation to conversation, making everyone smile as she raved about her own fiancé, who was apparently on a job—she didn't say what kind—but would be joining them the following week.

Pandora was a calm oasis. Whenever the room seemed to be heading toward frantic she smoothed the conversation with an easy word, a soft joke or in the case of her fiancé, a soothing touch.

Danita even briefly met Gabriel's Aunt Cynthia, who after confirming that Danita was registered in the state of California to vote, had spent ten minutes lecturing her on the necessity of energy reform. Danita was just as baffled as Gabriel that the woman would be at a party celebrating the wonders of new beginnings, fertility and spring.

Through it all, Gabriel and his father were mirror images of each other. Not only in looks, although Tobias had genetically blessed all three of his children with striking looks, especially his youngest son, but in attitude. Both smiled, charmed and interacted. And always held back.

It bothered her, a lot, that she found that fascinating in Gabriel. Because she damned well didn't want to find anything positive about a grifter like Tobias.

By the end of the evening, she wasn't sure if Gabriel was keeping her separate from his father on purpose or if it was just party happenstance, but she'd yet to share more than a dozen words with the man she'd come to town hoping to arrest.

Then again, that was about ten words more than Gabriel had shared with him.

"Danita, we put away most of the stock for the party. So you'll have to come back tomorrow," Pandora said as they each nibbled on the after-dinner cookies she'd set out. Her sweet serenity was a contrast to the more vivid, dynamic Black family. "I'd love to show you a few things. I have a sodalite sphere that I think will be perfect for you."

"Sodalite? Is that something you serve here in the café?" Danita asked with a hesitant smile.

"No." The other woman slipped a strand of smooth, auburn hair behind her ear as she laughed. "It's a stone. It's wonderful for clarity and inner peace. It's also great for seeing the truth and for building trust."

Danita's smile dimmed. Did she seem like she needed any of that? A little nervous, she smoothed one hand over the leather of her skirt. But before she could form the question, Pandora continued.

"The stone is a lovely blue that is a perfect match for your eyes," Pandora told her.

The knot in her stomach loosened as Danita accepted the invitation.

"This is a wonderful party. Do you have them often? I have to admit, I'm surprised to see Gabriel's entire family here," she said with a casual smile. "He said something about a little family tension, but I'm not seeing it."

Pandora's hazel eyes narrowed for just a second, like she was looking deep into Danita's soul. Then she shifted, pushing her hair behind her shoulder and gave a little shrug. "The store has eight gatherings a year. When the mayor suggested it, I agreed that it'd be fun to invite the townspeople now that I've taken over the store. A way of bringing everyone together."

"Maya's father must be thrilled to have her moving back. And Caleb too?" she said with a look of pure innocent curiosity. "Didn't Gabriel mention he'd just recently moved back as well?"

"Caleb came home to…visit," Pandora said, her hesitation so infinitesimal that only Danita's training picked it up. "He came into my store his first day home to see his dad, and, well, I guess our romance started there."

It was damned hard for Danita to accept that a woman whose face was lit with that much happiness and was practically overflowing with joy was lying to her. But there were too many tells. Tiny ones. The hesitation between words. A slight twitch of Pandora's fingers, loosely clasped on her lap. But why?

To protect the man she loved?

Danita's FBI resources offered plenty of information on Tobias Black, enough dirt on Gabriel Black, to make her attraction horribly uncomfortable and just a little info on Maya Black and her single arrest before she'd dropped off the map. But Caleb Black? The only information she'd found on him was brief mention in his father's file with his date of birth.

Why?

Hunter knew.

Her expression rapt and focused on Pandora as the other woman shared a few details of her and Caleb's courtship, Danita mulled over just what it was that Hunter knew. What was he keeping from her and why would it be necessary? And, the big question, how soon would she find out?

"I need to check the desserts, but I'll be right back." Pandora excused herself, waiting for Danita's nod before sliding gracefully to her feet.

Welcoming the brief alone-time, Danita's gaze shifted to the other side of the room.

It all came down to him.

Despite the fact that he was staying quiet and mellow from his position in a curvy iron chair in the corner, Tobias Black was clearly in charge of the room. And, she suspected, of whatever was really going on here.

The crime ring itself? Maybe.

Hunter's operation? Probably.

Was Tobias behind bringing all his family members together for his own purposes, regardless of whatever else was going on?

Most definitely.

Then Tobias's gaze landed on her. Speculation, admiration and just a hint of suspicion were clear in the dark blue depths. Before she could help herself, she arched one brow in challenge.

His eyes widened, then sparkled with laughter.

And with the grace of a man half his age, he rose and headed across the room.

Shit.

Danita's stomach dropped. Her nails dug into her palms as she tried to smooth her breathing. What was she thinking? She was here as the fake bimbo fiancée. Fake bimbos didn't issue challenges unless they involved Jell-O or tequila shooters.

She tried to align her thoughts and pull together all the threads of her control and her various roles.

Before Tobias could reach her, though, Gabriel stepped between them. With his back to her, all she could see was the breadth of his shoulders and, she sighed a little, the sweet view of his tight ass. Both looked a little tense, though.

"Sit down and relax, Gabriel. I just came over to get to know your friend. Not to share any family secrets," Tobias said. Then his grin turned crafty. "Or should I say, your fiancée? Isn't that how you introduced her to Caleb today?"

Danita wondered which comment had made Gabriel's shoulders stiffen. That his brother had ratted him out. Or that his dad had secrets on the mind.

"Maybe I'm not so crazy about Danita getting to know you, though," Gabriel shot back.

"Don't be silly," Danita broke in. "Of course I want to know your family, Gabriel, sweetie. That's why I'm here, silly boy."

She added a vapid smile and flirtatious flutter of her lashes to keep the rebuke from being obvious to anyone but Gabriel. His glare told her he'd got the message loud and clear. Tobias simply brushed his son aside to take a seat across from her.

"Well, let's chat then," he said with a smile that had enough edge to keep it from being fatherly, but was friendly enough not to be threatening. "Where are you from, Danita?"

"Bradford. That's a small town in Pennsylvania," she lied with a smile. "I moved to California hoping to be a star. You know, Hollywood with all its glitz and glamour, it was so appealing."

Standing behind his father's chair, Gabriel gave a rude eye roll.

"Indeed. Acting is a fine art. Are you focused on the big screen or the small?"

"Oh, neither," she said with a bubbly giggle, waving the options away with one hand. "I got here and within three months found out I was a horrible actress."

"That's too bad. But you stayed in California anyway? What are you doing now?"

"Well, I had to stay. I mean, my car broke down and I was pretty much out of money," she said with a helpless sort of shrug. "So I turned to Plan B."

"Well, now," Tobias said with an impressed sort of nod. "Backup plans are always clever. I'm impressed that you came out here with a dream and when you saw it wasn't going to work, you had an alternate. What's Plan B?"

"To be a singing sensation."

Gabriel wasn't quick enough to quell his laugh, but he did quickly turn it into a cough.

"You're a singer?" Tobias asked after blinking a couple of times.

"Well, no. I have a horrible voice. But I love the costumes," she said earnestly. "And I really thought they could kinda hide my voice. Synthesize it or something."

"Or something…" Gabriel snickered.

While Tobias shot a glare over his shoulder at his son, Danita worked up a pouty look. Jutting lower lip, puppy dog eyes and tucked-in chin.

"But they wouldn't. Not for me. I was really bummed," she said when the older man met her gaze again.

"That's a shame that you had to give up your second choice," Tobias said. She could see the glint of humor dancing in his eyes, just ahead of what might be suspicion. Whether he suspected her story, or suspected his son had horrible taste, didn't matter. Her story would stand. And Gabriel was the idiot who'd hauled her along as his fiancée instead of his bimbo, so his taste deserved to be questioned.

"It was a shame," she agreed.

"Did you give up on Hollywood then?"

"Oh, no," she said with a quick shake of her head. "I went to Disneyland."

"No place happier, right?"

"Right. Well, that and I got to be a princess there."

"Beg pardon?"

"I dressed up as a princess. I wore a gown and a tiara, waved to the kids and had my picture taken."

"You worked at the park?"

"Oh, no. They didn't give me a job. They said I didn't have the right look. But I did go every day for a week dressed as a princess, just to cheer myself up. It was great. And it got me over that whole star dream."

This was the point in her spiel that usually confused most people enough to start rubbing their temples and looking for an excuse to leave the discussion.

But not Tobias. He leaned forward, his hands hanging loose between his thighs. Laughter danced in his eyes.

The same laughter she saw reflected behind him in Gabriel's.

"So acting didn't pan out and singing was a disappointment. It sounds like you made a great princess. And what brought you this far north? You are living up here in Northern California now, right?"

Danita wet her lips. A warning shiver tingled down her spine. This shouldn't feel like a trap, but suddenly she felt like she should be stepping very, very carefully. This man was a criminal mastermind, she reminded herself. But she was a highly trained, very talented FBI agent. She could handle him.

"Danita's living with me," Gabriel interrupted.

What? She kept her expression clear and made sure her smile didn't waver. But what the hell was he trying to do? Was this some macho protect-the-little-woman thing? Or was he afraid she'd say something and ruin his game?

Either way, she wasn't letting him run roughshod over her. This was her case, dammit.

Before she could say anything, he continued. "I like keeping her…close."

"Is that a fact?" Tobias asked, his gaze never leaving Danita's face. She saw something in his eyes. Concern? Or triumph? It was gone too quickly for her to decide.

Danita narrowed her eyes, trying to read the subtext. Before she could catch a clue, though, Gabriel stepped around his father to offer her his hand. Without thinking, she slipped hers into it and let him pull her to her feet. He wrapped his arm around her shoulder and pulled her tight to the warm length of his body.

"We should go, Blondie."

She flicked a glance up at him. Then, noting the tension and what looked like sadness in his eyes, she frowned and, without thinking, slipped her arm around his waist to rub the small of his back in soothing circles.

As she turned to say goodbye to the group, he said in a voice meant for her ears only, "I think we need to have a little talk. In private."

Suddenly Danita didn't know what she wanted more.

To stay right here in this room filled with confusion and con artists.

Or to get back to the pseudo-privacy of their hotel room, and see just what Gabriel's *little talk* felt like.

6

"LOOK, I'D RATHER YOU didn't pour the extra dose of charm over my family."

Tossing her purse on the dresser, Danita gave him a puzzled look, then shrugged. "You brood in silence for the entire drive home, and that's the first thing you decide to say to me?"

Shoving his fists in the pockets of his slacks, Gabriel tried not to grit his teeth. He'd stayed silent on the ride home because he knew damned well if he made that demand aloud, he'd sound like a jackass. Always nice to be proved right.

"What's the big deal?" she continued, hanging her coat in the closet. "We're here to do a job. I'm here to prove your father is running this little crime ring. You're here to prove he isn't. Either way, we have to work together. And the faster we get it done, the better. People talk to people they like, so I was likeable."

His jaw had clenched when she mentioned her main objective—arresting his father. But he didn't comment. Instead, he asked, "Is that what you call it? Likeable?"

"Yes, that's exactly what I call it. You're acting like I hit on your father and tried to talk your brother and his fiancée into a threesome." Running her fingers through her hair as if to loosen the curls, and her fake persona, Danita gave him a long look, then pulled her largest suitcase out and laid it on the bed. The luggage distracted Gabriel's unexplainable frustration for a second as he watched her set the neatly folded stacks of clothes on the bed.

He tried not to drool over the bits of black lace and filmy red fabric that were surely something sexy. He didn't even need to see what it was to imagine that soft fabric draped over her pale, silky skin. His earlier frustration was quickly disappearing as desire rose.

Then she unzipped the bottom of the suitcase. Gabriel frowned, wondering what she was going to pull out of her FBI bag of tricks next. A cache of weapons? A computer station complete with homing signals and listening devices? Some weird but erotic form of bondage so she could tie him to the bed and ensure he didn't run off and get into trouble during the night?

Gabriel shifted, his hands fisting a little tighter in his pockets as his body stirred at the image. He'd never been a man to give up control, in any way, but the idea of playing tie-me-up with Danita was making him hard.

But what she pulled out of the bottom of the suitcase wasn't sexy or intriguing. It was big and squishy.

"Is that a sleeping bag?" he asked, squinting at the moss-green fabric.

She shot him an amused look as she rezipped the case and started stacking her clothes again. "What? You didn't think I was going to share a bed with you, did you?"

Gabriel grinned. "Is that a challenge?"

"Hardly," she said. But he saw the nerves in her eyes, in the way her fingers clenched the handle of the suitcase as she set it back in the closet. "Knowing our cover as a couple meant we'd have to share a room, I came prepared."

"You're going to bunk on the floor in a sleeping bag," he mocked. "Sounds comfy."

"It will be," she tossed back with a chilly smile. "Especially with the gun I'll have under my pillow."

"Is that for me, or for the bad guys?"

"That's for anyone who interrupts my sleep."

Gabriel's voice lowered to a husky purr. "Sweetheart, if I interrupt your sleep, you'll be thanking me. Not shooting me."

"Only in your dreams."

"You were a lot more fun when you were kissing my family's ass," he muttered, walking over to look out the window. He didn't know why her rejection bothered him, except that it did. Not in an ego-crushing way. He frowned at the dark view as he considered. No, it was more a hurt feelings kind of thing. Which was stupid. When had he started having feelings for her? And what the hell was wrong with him for letting that happen?

"Of course I was nice to your family. What's your problem with that? You're the one who claimed me as your fiancée instead of sex-for-hire," she reminded him. "All I did was play the part."

He glanced at the sleeping bag again and hunched his shoulders. Who the hell was she? The tough federal agent? The sweet girlfriend who'd charmed his family? Or the sexy siren who made a man so crazy he'd drop a few grand for a single kiss and then give thanks. Were they all parts she was playing? Who was the real Danita?

"You're damned good at playing," he muttered.

Eyes wide, she crossed her arms over her chest and jutted out her chin. "I beg your pardon?"

"How do women do that? Put so much disdain and ice in four simple words."

"How do men manage to walk upright with such huge egos cutting off their circulation?"

"As long as it's stroked nicely, my ego feeds my circulation."

Danita rolled her eyes, but he saw the flash of amusement in those blue depths.

"Look, we're stuck together for the rest of the week, so you might as well get over whatever's got you in a snit."

"And you need to start following the rules," she snapped back.

Sick of rules, sick of someone else calling the shots, Gabriel strode over, grabbed her shoulders and took her mouth in a quick, searing kiss. Her lips melted beneath his, soft and welcoming.

His body hardened. But before things could get interesting, she pressed her palms against his shoulders.

"This is crazy," she protested, pulling her mouth from his and stepping quickly away. So quickly, she almost tripped over her own feet and landed on the bed. She grabbed the footboard for balance with one hand while shoving the other through her hair. Taking a deep breath, she shook her head in protest.

"Crazy," she repeated. "You need to stop doing that. I'm a federal agent. You're in my custody. Quit," she stopped, as if she'd run out of words. Instead she waved her hand in the air to indicate whatever had happened before and grimaced. "Just quit."

"But I like it," he said with a grin as he leaned against the headboard and crossed his arms over his chest. He liked her all flustered and out of control, too. The more confused she was, the more confident he was that he was in charge of this little game. And as his daddy had taught him when he was young, confidence was key to everything.

He stepped closer, trapping her between the footstool and

the hard length of his own…body. His muscles tensed, hardening right along with his dick as he watched her breath shudder. Her pupils were huge as she ran her tongue along the lush deliciousness of her lower lip.

His eyes narrowed, taking in the rapid pulse fluttering against the delicate line of her throat, the gorgeous sight of her nipples pebbling against the soft fabric of her black sweater. She was incredible.

And he was going to have her.

Keeping his hands to himself, he leaned in, brushing a soft whisper of a kiss against the pulse pounding in her throat. She moaned. He leaned back and grinned.

"Get a grip, Black. We're here to do a job," she reminded him, her words coming out in a gasp. "You're just getting carried away with the roles we're playing."

"Roles?"

"Right. This isn't real," she claimed, sounding desperate. He figured she was trying to convince herself as much as him. "None of this is real."

"Didn't you hear? The food at that little gathering was all made up of aphrodisiacs," he said, his fingers sliding along the silky-smooth curve of her cheek before tangling in her soft blond curls. "You know the thing about aphrodisiacs? They don't create desire. They amplify it."

Her breath shuddered, washing over his lips like a soft caress.

"So baby, all this heat between us? Those oysters and asparagus, the chocolate and cayenne, they're just turning up that heat. And that heat is real. Do you like how it feels? Aren't you curious about how much better it'll be when it hits a boiling point?"

This time he pressed his lips to the delicate line of her jaw, whispering tiny open-mouthed kisses all the way to her ear, where he blew softly before nipping at the soft flesh of her earlobe.

Her tiny mewl of approval made his dick dance with happy joy. Damn, she was responsive. This was going to be one hell of a hot night.

Before he could step things up, though, she gave a little moan. Then she pushed him away. Again. Gabriel bit back a growl of frustration. "That's crazy. There is no such thing as aphrodisiacs. Just like there's nothing between us. Circumstance and proximity don't equal true attraction."

Amusement faded along with the tentative shift he'd made into a good mood. Anger, frustration and an unexplainable sadness overwhelmed him again.

"Blondie, you are one hell of a lousy actress for a professional liar."

"You're the professional liar," she snapped, sidestepping him and hurrying over to the dresser so the wide expanse of the room was safely between them. "And I save all my acting skills to pretend I'm attracted to you when we're around other people."

Gabriel had no idea why, but he was suddenly furious. He hadn't signed on for this lousy game. He'd lost a cool mil already because of the sexy blonde standing there, and now she was telling him she didn't feel this intense, wild attraction between them. He'd had to face down his entire family, knowing they were all in jeopardy and the futures they were so happily planning could easily be screwed to hell if he wasn't careful.

And now, the woman whose mouth had melted under his not two minutes ago was claiming she had to pretend to be attracted to him.

She was going to deny the heat he'd felt? The way she responded to him? Pretend it was all about the job?

Well, screw that.

Thoroughly fed up with all of the lies, all of the pretenses, Gabriel grabbed Danita's forearms and lifted her off her feet.

"What the—"

Before she could finish spewing her outrage, he pushed her back against the wall and trapped her body there with his own. The hard planes of his chest pressed against her soft curves, his thighs nestled so tight between hers that he knew damned well she could feel his dick hardening against her.

He took her mouth. All the fury, the frustration he felt poured into the kiss. There was no apology on his lips, no gentle request in his actions. It was pure demand.

His tongue thrust, his hands clenched. He pulled her tight against his body, letting the feel of her curves send him even higher.

Her fingernails dug into his shoulders. Her lips danced against his, her tongue tangling temptingly. He felt like his body was set to boil. Desire, sharp and a little edgy, gripped him in a tight fist.

His hands tightened on her waist and he lifted, settling her on the dresser and angling himself between her thighs. Scooting closer, she gasped as her skirt slid higher. Gabriel wanted to touch that sweet flesh, needed to taste the soft curve of her thighs. But he couldn't.

Not yet.

"I don't want to stop," he admitted breathlessly. "If you're going to make me, you'd damned well better do it now."

Her eyes, huge and blue, glistened with emotions that Gabriel could only guess at. Desperation clawed at him. Needs roared through his system, both sexual and emotional.

But he waited.

Because when he took her, it was going to be incredible. Better than either of them had ever experienced before in their lives. And he'd be damned if she was going to ruin it with some lame excuse tomorrow morning.

Danita's heart pounded so hard her chest hurt. Her breath came in pants. Her body tingled with needs so intense, she thought she was going to explode.

"Well?" Gabriel demanded, his gold eyes narrow with desire.

Desire for her.

Not the real her. He only saw the role she played. Or... roles? She'd played so many with him, they were all blurring. But none were her. Hell, she didn't even know who the real her was anymore.

All the reasons to say no flashed through her mind. There was no solid, practical reason not to shove him away and demand that they return to a professional standing.

But her body, damn her body, it wanted more.

Needed more.

Demanded more.

"This is a mistake," she said, her words so soft they were barely there.

"What fun is life without a few mistakes here and there?" His fingers trailed, so softly they were barely touching, the elastic lace of her stockings where they met her thighs. Danita shuddered as excitement swirled through her. Her brain fogged, overwhelmed by desire.

She leaned closer.

"It's going to cost us," she predicted breathlessly, her lips just inches from his. So close, she could almost taste him.

"Nothing worth having is free," he said, his eyes locked on hers. He was waiting, she knew, for her to finish making the move. For her to take responsibility for this next step.

Nerves were there. Clawing and poking at her confidence. But desire was stronger. Need was predominant.

She had to taste him.

Had to feel him.

Had to have him.

Now.

Like she was jumping off a high cliff to her probable death, Danita closed her eyes and took the plunge. Her lips met his in a soft, damp slide, making Gabriel groan.

Power, bigger and darker than anything she'd ever felt on the job, spiked through her system. That she could make a man as desirable and gorgeous and dangerous as Gabriel Black groan, that was a major rush.

Just what else could she make him do?

She slipped her tongue between his lips, sliding it along his, swirling, enticing. His fingers tightened on her waist, then, as if unable to help himself, he poured himself into the kiss. Their tongues tangled and danced. Their lips devoured, pressing first one way, then the other.

Her nipples tightened with need, the soft satin of her bra torture against the aching flesh. As if hearing their plea, Gabriel's hands quit teasing her thighs to graze their way up her torso until he reached the heavy weight of her breasts. Fingers curved over her sweater, cupping the aching mounds and squeezing gently. Danita whimpered deep in her throat as the move sent a shaft of desire swirling low in her belly. Her thighs quivered, damp heat pooling between her legs.

Those magic hands skimmed down, gently caressing her torso and leaving a trail of tingling delight until he reached the edge of her sweater. Anticipation tangled with nerves, adding a wonderfully addictive layer of delight to the sexual tension spreading through her body.

Slowly, so slow she wanted to tear her mouth from his and urge him to hurry, Gabriel raised her sweater. Cool air washed over her heated skin. He released her lips, leaning back just enough to pull her top the rest of the way off. As if she were hypnotized, Danita raised her hands overhead to make it easier to give him more access to her body.

As soon as the fabric cleared her fingers, she was reaching

for him again. But Gabriel stepped back with a tiny shake of his head. His eyes traveled over her like an art lover might gaze at the Mona Lisa. With pleasure, excitement and just a little bit of awe. Her smile was just a little shaky at the corners. She'd never had anyone look at her like that. It was intoxicating.

Her head swimming in the delight of his admiration, Danita reached for him again. This time, Gabriel gave in to her demand, his mouth closing over hers.

This was amazing. Delicious. The most incredible feeling she'd ever had.

That little voice in the corner of her mind, the one that usually kept her from being shot in the back, was screaming a warning, though. This was against the rules.

Gabriel's hands cupped her breasts, sliding over the slick satin fabric as he gently squeezed.

To hell with rules, she thought as she moaned.

But the rules were what had made her the woman she was, that irritating voice reminded. A woman she admired. So she couldn't completely ignore them.

"We shouldn't," she protested. It was a pathetic protest, she knew, since her fingers were making quick work of the buttons of his shirt as she spoke. But she had to say the words aloud if she was going to face herself in the morning.

"Yeah, yeah," he muttered, those gorgeous eyes watching intently as his fingers skimmed along the satin edge of her bra, dipping beneath the fabric to tease the rock hard tip of her breast before sliding to the other side. "The time for half-assed excuses already passed."

This kiss was even more intense. Like hot molten passion pulling her in. She shuddered, her body melting as his fingers tweaked her aching nipple before sliding away again. She wanted him so bad. Wanted to feel everything he had to offer. To see if it was as good as she was imagining. But that didn't mean she was abdicating all control and letting Gabriel be in charge, here.

"This is a big deal," she protested, pulling her lips from his only to have him start kissing his way down her throat. His lips were soft, his tongue hot. She swore even her toes were melting. Still, she had to take a stand, feeble though it might be. "We do this, and everything changes. I think, maybe, we should slow down."

Except she didn't want to.

"You think too much," he decided. She barely saw the warning in his eyes before he thrust his hands into her hair to tilt her head back. Just before his mouth took hers, he said, "Obviously I'm not pushing the right buttons to shut off your brain. Yet."

Uh-oh.

Gabriel kissed her as if his life depended on blowing her mind. His hands left her hair, one slipping between her shoulder blades to unsnap her bra as the other reached down to shove her skirt higher. Her breath came in pants, her head spinning at the pace he set.

Fast, furious and intense.

Fingers tweaked her nipples, first one then the other. In a quick tug, he ripped her damp panties, the sound of tearing satin echoing loudly through the room. Her thighs quivered and her heart raced.

"Oh my…" Her words trailed off against his still plundering mouth as Gabriel's fingers found her wet, throbbing core.

Without a second of hesitation, he dove right in. She couldn't hold back her whimper when his finger trailed along her swollen bud.

At the same time, his fingers teased her nipple, preparing it for the wet heat of his mouth. His tongue swirled, sucking and nipping, making her moan as the combined torments sent her body screaming for release.

How many damned hands did he have?

Her own fingers tunneled into his hair, clutching the dark strands for support as the world spun out of control. She wanted to touch him. She wanted to explore his body the same way he was delighting hers.

But all she could do was hold on and enjoy the ride.

Which was clearly fine with Gabriel.

His tongue traced a sweet homage around her areola as his fingers danced over her swollen nether flesh. She was sliding into the gentle delight he was giving her body when he changed the game.

Suddenly his teeth nipped at her nipples, making her gasp and shudder. His fingers thrust, one then two, fast and hot into her body, making her cry out in delight. Her juices flowed, hot and inviting. She moved against him, wanting more. Needing more.

It was like he'd lit a fire within her. Her body burned. She had to fan the flames and take this higher. Hotter. She shoved his shirt off his shoulders, not caring that it caught on his biceps because his hands were so busy. She needed to touch flesh. Her fingers scraped the hard breadth of his muscled shoulders and she purred deep in her throat at the strength there. For a man who talked his way in and out of fortunes and trouble, he was amazingly built.

He sucked her nipple into his mouth, swirling his tongue around the turgid flesh as his fingers danced faster. She let her head fall back, her body arched into his.

"Oh, God," she breathed as every muscle in her body tightened, as the pleasure became so intense she could barely breathe.

"Grab it, babe," he muttered against her breast. "Grab on, and ride."

His voice, low and husky, triggered her release. Danita's head fell back against the mirror, her entire body tightening as the climax ripped through her. Her fingers dug into his shoulders as she gripped him, holding on as if Gabriel were the only thing that still existed in her world.

Slowly, deliciously, she floated on waves of pleasure. Gabriel's touch was now soothing instead of titillating. His kisses soft whispers over her sensitized flesh. His mouth took hers in the sweetest of kisses as the last shudder of her climax rippled through her body.

Before she could do more than gasp with delight, Gabriel moved. Her body shivered without his heat, sagging into the unwielding hardness of the dresser.

She barely had her eyes open, and definitely hadn't regained the power of thought, before he moved. She watched him rip open a condom and wanted to reach out and take the pleasure of sheathing him, but he moved so fast, she didn't have a chance.

Two heartbeats later and he was back, his body hard and strong between her still shaking thighs. Danita wanted to say something. To do something to indicate how good she felt. To make him feel just as wonderful.

But Gabriel was clearly not in a chatty mood. His mouth took hers in a devouring sort of kiss. Even as she was gasping and sinking into the spiraling delight, his body thrust into hers.

"Oh, God," she said again, mewling in delight as his hard length filled her. He was so big. So strong.

She wrapped her legs around his hips, her feet digging into the hard planes of his butt and realized she still had her black patent leather pumps on.

Snickering a little, her lashes fluttered open to see him staring at her, his gold eyes so intent it was like he was trying to see into her soul.

Feeling more naked than ever, Danita tried to look away. But he was a sorcerer holding her in a spell, he wouldn't release her gaze. She couldn't look away. Couldn't hide from the powerful heat burning between them.

He drove into her body, flesh pounding flesh in a mesmerizing rhythm, each thrust sending her higher, spinning her body tighter.

His fingers slipped between their bodies, teasing and tweaking her swollen nub. The caress sent Danita flying over the edge. Her body exploded. The orgasm ripped through her like a tidal wave, pouring and pounding pleasure into every pore. Her breath came in pants. Her hair, damp with sweat, stuck to her face as she flew.

Her gaze still locked on his, she saw his eyes narrow, then with the most exquisite look of pleasure in those gold depths, she watched him tumble over the edge. His groan was guttural and deep. His body so tight, she could see the muscles ripple as he tried to hold back.

Needing, desperately, a little of the power he'd shown over her, Danita arched her body. Her heels dug into his hips, her breasts brushed a sizzling trail over his chest. His groan deepened. His eyes were almost black as the pupils expanded.

"Grab it, babe," she said, tossing his earlier words back at him at the same time she leaned back so there was just enough space between their bodies to put on a show. Balancing on her hips, her eyes locked on his, she reached up with both hands to cup her own breasts, offering herself to him.

His eyes contracted. His body jerked. His movements grew jerky, fast, then slow. Then he slammed into her with a guttural cry of delight.

They fell into each other's arms, both breathing fast as they tried to calm their racing hearts.

"Let's try that again," he breathed against her hair.

She shouldn't. Oh, God, she couldn't believe what they'd just done. How unprofessional—but delicious—it had been. She was crazy. This was crazy. But the incredible sensations pouring through her body said otherwise. Danita looked into Gabriel's gorgeous eyes and sighed. She was already in trouble. Might as well make whatever price she paid really worthwhile.

"With pleasure," she finally purred.

7

A BOUT OF HOT, WILD sex should have a man waking up with a big, fat smile on his face. A couple of orgasms, a handful of panting exclamations to his prowess as a love god and the smile should be just this side of smug.

Propped on one elbow, the sheet pooled at his waist, Gabriel glared at the tousled blond hair barely visible above the mossy green fabric of the sleeping bag. They'd barely finished their second round of wild sex, Gabriel's heart was still racing, and she'd climbed off his body with a distant smile, grabbed prurient flannel pajamas out of her suitcase and locked herself in the bathroom.

Ten minutes later, she came out with her face washed clean, her hair a smooth halo around her pretty face, and a wall a mile thick around her. With a murmured good-night, she'd grabbed that damned sleeping bag, made a show of taking her gun from her purse, then snagged a pillow off the armchair. Before Gabriel could yank his jaw off his chest, she'd settled the sleeping bag in front of the door like she was some kind of guard dog and settled down to sleep.

He'd be damned if he was going to beg her to sleep with him. But still, he felt cheated out of his smug morning-after smile.

He eyed the tousle-haired temptation snuggled up in that sleeping bag dreaming her cozy dreams and debated.

He could wake her up. Just haul her out of there, trap her against the wall and pour all his frustrations into her body while making her scream in ecstasy.

Or he could take the oh-so-subtle hint from her body language, all curled up facing away from him, and leave her the hell alone.

Before he could decide whether to let this game play out or to yank her from that damned sleeping bag and earn his smile, the phone rang.

Danita didn't stir.

Either she was a really deep sleeper, a questionable trait for an FBI agent on assignment.

Or she'd been awake all along.

"Black," Gabriel snapped into the receiver.

"Morning, big brother," Maya sang out in an annoyingly cheerful voice. "I didn't interrupt anything important, did I?"

He watched Danita as she turned over to face him, pushing that sunshine-bright hair off her face and giving him a questioning look.

"Nope," he dismissed. "Nothing important going on here."

"Ooh," Maya said, drawing out the word in her typical annoying little sister way.

"Cut it out," Gabriel told her, shoving the blankets off and climbing, naked, out of bed. Danita's sleep-swollen eyes widened, her breath catching in an almost silent moan of appreciation.

Maybe he'd find something to smile about this morning after all. Gabriel arched one brow in a silent offer. Blushing, Danita tugged her sleeping bag higher as if she were the one strutting around nude.

He knew he was acting like a pouty little boy who insisted on taking his toys home because the other kids didn't want to play with them. But he didn't care. Gabriel tucked the phone between his ear and shoulder and yanked his jeans up. He didn't bother to zip or snap them,

"What's up?" he asked Maya. "Did you need me for something?"

Whether it was because she felt vulnerable huddled in a sleeping bag while he strode around nude, or if it was her way to avoid looking at him, Danita climbed out of her puffy bed.

"Actually, I was calling for Danita."

His gaze sliced across the room, watching the woman in question tuck her gun back in her purse and neatly fold the sleeping bag into a smaller puff of fabric. He was sure she'd hide it back in her suitcase, too.

"Hang on," he snapped before tossing the phone onto the puffy gateway of Danita's sleeping bag.

"Hello?" Danita greeted hesitantly, her gaze flickering away from Gabriel's as if she were afraid that a full-on look would mean she had to give him a morning blow job.

"Today? Um…" She grimaced, finally looking directly at him with her eyes wide and insistent. "I think Gabriel had plans for the day, actually."

He did, but he'd much rather execute them without an FBI audience. He still wasn't crazy about Danita pouring on the charm to con his family, but figured they were all savvy enough to handle themselves. Mostly because this was too good an opportunity to pass up.

So instead of taking Danita's hint, he gave her a wicked smile and said loud enough to carry through the phone line, "Nope. The day is wide-open, babe. Go ahead and have fun."

Her glare was lethal. Blue eyes, free of the heavy makeup he'd seen her wear so far, were laser-sharp with anger.

But her tone stayed light and friendly as she answered Maya's onslaught of questions.

"I really shouldn't," she protested for the third time. "I don't have a gift or anything."

She listened, still glaring at Gabriel, then gave a silent sigh. "Well, if you're sure, then yes. Of course. I'd love to come to Pandora's bridal shower this afternoon."

Well, that freed up his afternoon nicely, Gabriel grinned. Now he could poke into the goon squad's plans, see what he could uncover about their revered leader without Danita and her cop sensibilities getting in his way.

It also meant leaving his family to Danita's mercy. His grin faded. Crap.

He strode over to Danita, holding out his hand for the phone. "I need to talk to Maya before you hang up."

Giving him a long, calculating look, Danita's lips quirked in challenge. She turned her back on him to finish saying her goodbyes, a clear message that she still thought she was in charge. Then, without looking at him again, she held out the phone. As soon as he took it, she went to her suitcase, gathered clothes, grabbed a bag and sauntered off to the bathroom.

"What's Caleb doing while his bride-to-be gets her party on?" he asked his sister.

"He's fixing the porch on his new place, remember?" she said. "You should have stuck around longer last night so you could see it. It's really sweet, just a couple blocks from Aunt Cynthia's. Caleb said as soon as he's done with the house renovations, he's going to build a big fence to keep her out, though."

Over Maya's laughter about how disagreeable their aunt could be, Gabriel heard the shower start. That didn't mean Danita might not have her ear pressed to the door, but still, it made eavesdropping more difficult.

"Hey," he said quietly into the phone, interrupting Maya's

bemoaning the constant campaign pitches from the mayor. "Keep your guard up today, okay?"

The silence was alive with questions. He waited, trying to anticipate the direction his inquisitive sister would take them, and just how he'd answer without blowing his con and Danita's cover.

"You're afraid your sweetie might learn a few family secrets?" Maya guessed. Then her tone turned from teasing to deadly serious. "You're not really planning a long-term relationship with her without telling her the truth about the family, are you? I mean, she has to know what you, well, do. Right?"

Gabriel huffed out a breath and dropped to the bed. Well, he hadn't expected her to go in that direction. *Shit.*

"I just don't want to wave our history, or any current activities, in Danita's face," he finally said.

"You know you can't build a relationship on a lie," Maya said quietly. "If you're really planning to marry her, you have to be honest. You have to tell her who you are, Gabriel. The real you. Not some character you're playing to pull a con."

Good thing he wasn't really planning to marry her, then. Because he didn't particularly like the idea of letting anyone, especially someone with a badge, know who he really was.

"Don't worry about it," he suggested. "Just, you know, focus on the girly wedding stuff today instead of heart-to-heart confessions."

"You sure? Because I'd planned on hauling out the photo album and showing her all of your baby pictures. Especially that one of you, naked, playing in the mud. What were you? Four?"

"Behave, Maya," he ordered, laughing now. "Just, you know, keep it smooth, okay?"

"I was thinking I'd do the family dinner thing tonight. You'll come, right? Spend some time with Dad."

The shower stopped. Gabriel puffed out a breath, staring out the window at the thick copse of pines. He hadn't realized until last night how much he missed his father. His entire family. He had no desire to move back to bucolic Black Oak. But he didn't want to shut the door to visits. But until he'd tied up this mess, he couldn't plan for any of that.

"No," he decided. Distance was better. Until he'd figured out who was setting Tobias up, at least. "I've got plans tonight."

He offered an absent goodbye as he gathered his own clothes for the day, and his thoughts for the next state in the game. He needed an ally. Someone in the goon squad who could clue him in to the bigger picture. He knew he wasn't going to get the name of the kingpin, but he might garner enough info to develop some kind of plan.

"All yours," Danita said as she exited the steamy bathroom, the scent of wildflowers filling the air.

Gabriel wasn't a man who looked for subtlety in women. He'd always found that the more obvious a woman, the easier she was to deal with. So Danita's hair slicked back, her face bare, her wholesome image shouldn't appeal to him.

So why the hell did she?

"Did you have sweet dreams?" he asked, on edge and wanting her to join him.

"Let's not play games, okay?" she said, giving him a direct look at odds with the sexy memory he had from the previous night. "We had sex. It's over. Now we'll set it aside and forget about it."

"What if I don't want to forget it?" he asked, both irritated and admiring of her poise.

Her only response was a casual shrug as she tucked her jammies and whatever else back into her suitcase. The fabric of her dress, a soft blue that perfectly matched her eyes, stretched over her hips, making him damn near drool and shoving him just a little closer to that edge.

"What'll you be doing while I'm enjoying tea and petit fours while toasting your brother's upcoming wedding?" she asked as she held up two pair of shoes, one a strappy purple, the other vivid blue. Both made a strong argument for the allure of foot fetishes. "Helping your brother build a porch, was it?"

He shook his head, deciding to focus on the admiration instead of irritation at her intent focus on pretending they hadn't blown each other's minds the night before. Fine. She wanted casual, he could play casual like nobody's business.

"Nah. I'm better at tearing things down than hammering them together." Still, he could see she wanted an answer. Taking his time, he selected a shirt, then grabbed underwear. Danita's gaze cut from the black boxers in his hand to his unbuttoned, unzipped jeans and her breath hitched.

Desire flared in her blue eyes, giving Gabriel a brief hope that they could stop pretending and have some sweet a.m. follow-up to their hot night.

Then she blinked and it was gone. Instead she gave him a questioning look. "So what'll you do instead? Visit your father? Read a book? Scam a few old ladies?"

"I'm more interested in scamming younger ladies." Gabriel grinned. "I figured I'd hang out here. Make nice with the goon squad. Tour the grounds, see what kind of changes Ham's made around here since I moved away."

Her eyes narrowed. "What are you up to?"

Smart woman.

Deciding he'd rather ignore her question than lie to her, Gabriel shrugged. Before she could ask anything else, he strode over until he was within touching distance. Close enough for the wildflower sweetness of her perfume to wash over him. Close enough to see her pulse flutter at the base of her throat. And, thankfully, close enough to see her nipples bead against the soft fabric of her dress.

"You forgot something," he murmured, desperately craving a taste of her again.

"What?"

He tossed his clothes on the dresser behind her, then before she could move, slipped his hands into her damp hair. His fingers curved over the back of her head, tilting her face up to meet his.

The kiss was a sweet hello. His lips brushed over hers, sipping gently. Coaxing nicely. When she rewarded him with a moan, he took it deeper. His tongue swirled. Their breath mingled. His body hardened in demand.

But this wasn't the time.

There was a bigger game at stake. A game he intended to win. And, he decided in that second as their tongues danced sweetly together, Danita was going to be his prize for a game well played.

He slowly, oh so slowly, released her lips. Eyes still closed to hold on to those last vestiges of delight, he sighed. His fingers, still tangled in her damp tresses, clenched tight for just a second, unwilling to let go. Then he forced his eyes open and his body to relax.

"You forgot to kiss me good morning," he said with an easy smile, pretending that little meeting of the lips hadn't kicked his ass harder than all the lovemaking the night before.

"And you're out of line," Danita said, her voice shaky. "We're here to do a job. The whole lovers thing is only supposed to be an act. Our cover. You need to stop."

She stepped away, took a deep breath and finally met his eyes. Confusion and stress were clear in hers. "You need to stop," she repeated. "We're going to screw this job up. Someone will get hurt if we don't focus and stay on track.

That someone could be you. It could be me. Or it could be a member of your family. Are you willing to risk that?"

Gabriel gave her a searching look before gathering his clothes. When he reached the bathroom door, he glanced back. She was staring, worry clear in those pretty blue eyes.

"I'll finish the job, Blondie. And I'll win the game with zero casualties. And when I'm done?" His smile was cocky and assured, because he knew he was making this promise to both of them. "When this is done, it's just going to be you and me. No excuses, no games, no bullshit. And no more running away."

GABRIEL'S VOW, because those hadn't been idle words, was still ringing in Danita's head three hours later as she walked up the cobblestone path toward the Black Oak Inn. Her thighs were sore from her unexpected workout the night before, bruises from their foray against the dresser keeping her aware of just what she'd done with Gabriel. And how damned good it had felt.

Too good. She'd had to force herself out of his arms before she'd begged him for more. She'd grabbed onto that sleeping bag like it was a lifeline. Compartmentalizing, she told herself. Keeping the sex from being too important. *Or running scared,* the little voice in the back of her head mocked.

And now it was time to pretend to be the loving fiancée. Quite a different role than the good-time girl she'd come to town as. She smoothed a nervous hand over the soft jersey material of her blue dress. The fabric relied on her figure for its style, flowing in a smooth flow from the sweetheart neckline to her calves. She'd dressed it up for the shower with a dozen bangles that climbed halfway up one long sleeve, and a vivid turquoise chiffon scarf twisted around her waist in lieu of a belt. Purple sandals and a matching headband tied the ladylike look together nicely.

Now to act the part she'd dressed for. She grabbed the door handle, her last-minute gift in the other hand and with a deep breath, stepped into bride central with a big smile on her face.

Ten minutes later, she wished she was still meeting with the gang of armed goons. At least then she'd understood the rules. She definitely didn't belong in this roomful of giggling women, all talking about lingerie, trading recipes and singing odes to true love.

"You look like you're ready to run from the room."

"Of course not," Danita lied, offering Cassiopeia a big smile. Pandora's mother looked like a Celtic gypsy with a crystal fetish. Red curls waved over the shoulders of a green velvet caftan, clashing wonderfully with the string of pink crystals around her neck. "It's a lovely party. I'm just a little shy is all."

The redhead arched one slender brow and tilted her head. She looked at Danita like she could see clear through to her soul and was taking notes. "Sweetheart, you don't have a shy bone in your body. But you are uncomfortable with all of this. Estrogen overload, I'm thinking. You must work with men, hmm?"

Warning signals rang in Danita's head, but she kept her expression light and her laugh easy. "Oh, no. I work in a dress boutique in San Francisco, actually."

"Hmmm." Green eyes appraised her, then Cassiopeia took her hand. After a brief glance at Danita's palm, the woman stared into her eyes.

Her shoulders a little stiffer now, Danita briefly wished for some kind of woo-woo shield she could wrap around her.

"Come with me, sweetheart," Cassiopeia commanded before Danita could figure out how to get away. "I wasn't going to do readings, this is Pandora's day, after all. But you clearly need some insight and guidance."

"No, thank you, though." Danita believed in the esoteric arts just enough that her nerves were dancing with objections. "I should say hi to Pandora. And to Maya, she just came in with more of those lovely chocolate tarts."

Her hand firmly gripping Danita's, Cassiopeia plowed through the crowd like a friendly steamship. "Don't be silly. You'll have plenty of time to enjoy tarts after the reading."

But after a quick glance at Danita's stressed face, she made a beeline for the tarts, tucking three into a plate and handing it over without letting go of her other hand.

"Sit, sit," she said when they'd arrived at a small cubby off of the dining room. She pulled a velvet pouch from a pocket, then unwrapped a thick deck of cards as Danita cautiously sank into a tapestry-covered chair, her tarts still in hand.

"Cassiopeia, I appreciate the offer," Danita said with a smile as she set the plate on the small table. "But I'll admit, this kind of thing kind of scares me. I think I'd much rather wait and see what life has to offer as it happens. I don't want to ruin the surprise."

"Oh, I don't think there will be too many surprises here," Cassiopeia said with a knowing smile, shuffling the large cards with deft fingers. "We're not looking to the future so much as we're taking a more in-depth look at the present."

"All I need is a mirror for that."

"Then consider this a magnifying mirror."

Through shuffling, she offered the deck to Danita. Not seeing any way out of the reading, Danita swallowed hard, then schooled her face to smooth calm.

"Cut the deck into three, please."

Danita was pleased that her fingers didn't tremble when she lifted half the deck and set it next to the remaining half.

Cassiopeia took the cards back, restacking them, then dealt the top six into a triangle with the seventh in the center.

"Influences. Past, present and future. The Five of Swords

and Strength. Eight of Cups with The Lovers. And Death with the Two of Cups. Your lesson is the Seven of Cups."

Danita barely heard Cassiopeia's husky words, she was so fixated on the naked card. *The Lovers?* Shit. It was like someone had plastered a sticker reporting how many orgasms Gabriel had given her last night.

"You've had a difficult past," Cassiopeia was saying in that singsong tone. "A childhood subjected to talk and gossip, that while it gave you something of a complex, it also made you a strong, empowered woman. You've developed a tendency to hide from your past behind that strength, though. Until you face it, you can't move forward."

Danita's eyes flew from the naked couple card to Cassiopeia's knowing green eyes. Her heart sped up, making it a struggle to keep her expression neutral. She didn't believe in this stuff, she reminded herself. Not really.

"The Eight of Cups and The Lovers mark where you are on your present journey. You've an opportunity to leave the past behind on your search for something. Your quest will allow you to overcome emotional baggage, but it will require you to trust as you've never done before."

"What trust?" Danita asked before she could help herself. There was probably something telling in the fact that the Lovers card scared her a lot more than the Death one. "That's The Lovers card. Doesn't it mean sex?"

Perfectly groomed brows arched over amused eyes. "No, darling. The Lovers is so much more than sex. It's balance. It's choice. It's finding love."

Even as tiny tendrils of panic clutched at her, Danita was shaking her head. "Oh, no. I'm don't believe in—"

She barely managed to stop herself before blurting out the word *love.* Not a good confession given that she was here pretending to be engaged. Dammit, being a good-time-girl was so much easier.

Flustered, Danita sucked in a deep breath, forcing herself to remember that she wasn't here to discuss her psyche, she was here to break a crime ring. But her eyes were drawn to that Death card as dread curled low in her belly.

"This indicates change," Cassiopeia instructed, one red-tipped finger pointing to the hooded skeleton. "The end of one phase of your life, and the beginning of another. The release of something painful that you've carried with you for years. In order to move forward, you have to let go."

But what if she was scared to move forward? Danita couldn't tear her eyes off the card.

"Excuse me?"

Jolting, both women glanced toward the door. Cassiopeia in outrage, Danita with gratitude. Maya gave an artful grimace before offering an apologetic "Cassiopeia, the caterer is ready to bring out Pandora's cake. I thought you'd want to be there."

Cassiopeia's irritation faded as she glanced at her watch before gathering the cards together and dumping them, cloth and all, into her pocket. "They aren't supposed to bring the cake out for an hour yet. What is that girl thinking?"

She gave Danita an apologetic look, "I'm sorry, darling. We'll finish this later, okay?"

Danita offered a weak smile. It was like a steamroller apologizing for not completely smooshing you.

"You looked like you needed to be rescued," Maya said with a laugh after the redhead had swept out of the room. "Don't let Cassiopeia freak you out. Whatever she sees, she keeps it to herself. She's better at that confidentiality thing than most doctors."

"She's…" *Scary. Freakishly accurate. Intimidating.* "She's fun."

"She's going crazy with the wedding stuff, actually," Maya confessed. "Dad insisted on paying for the entire wedding, so she's trying to keep the balance by throwing a couple of weeks' worth of parties and celebrations."

Danita looked back at the table where her future had just terrified her and grimaced. "Couldn't he have let her bake a cake instead?"

Maya laughed, but before she could say anything, a forbidding looking woman called to her.

"Damn." Maya's curse was more a breath than a word. Her smile didn't change, but her body stiffened as the older lady approached. "Danita, have you met my aunt? Cynthia Parker, also known as Her Honor, the Mayor. Aunt Cynthia, this is Danita."

"Yes, yes, we've met. You're a registered voter, as I recall?" Cynthia said with a toothy smile. "Tell me, what issues are important to you in the election next fall? Are you a proponent of gun control? How do you feel we're doing, as a country, with the war on drugs?"

Huh? Danita's eyes cut to Maya, who had a look of resigned amusement on her face. The younger woman gave a shrug and rolled her eyes as if to say *ignore her.*

"Mrs. Parker, I'm sorry but I'm not sure I'll still be living in the state next fall." Or that she wanted to dish politics at a bridal shower.

The mayor's brown eyes narrowed, disappointment clear on her face. Then she visibly regrouped and gave a friendly nod. "I understand. You have doubts about your future with my nephew. With good reason, of course. He's the epitome of his father. Oh, the charm is there, but the problems that go along with it are plentiful. If you manage to stay together through fall, you and I will have a chat about your background."

With that and a pat on Danita's shoulder, the mayor strode away.

Relieved to see her go, and baffled by the bitterness in her tone when she'd mentioned Gabriel, Danita frowned.

"I'm confused," Danita confessed to Maya. "She sounded like she had a problem with Gabriel. And that part about discussing my background. Was that a joke?"

"More like a test. Aunt Cynthia is fanatical about the family name. She figures Dad's done enough to damage it. Then you factor in Caleb and Gabriel both being wild troublemakers as teens and she's spent years trying to overcome the blight our side of the family has cast on her political aspirations."

Must be rough living down reputations like the Blacks'. Danita wondered if the good mayor had a clue just how bad those reputations really were.

She spent the next few hours trying to find out. She talked to guests. To friends of the family and townspeople alike. Everyone had good things to say about the Black family, and the bad they shared was always tempered by indulgent laughter.

By three o'clock the bridal shower was over and Danita's head was so full she was ready to explode from information overload. It was like attending a briefing session with a group of magpies all hopped up on champagne, chocolate and pre-wedding sex talk.

She left with her arms filled with a basket of bath product she'd won playing the lingerie game, a box with leftover cake she'd been instructed to share with Gabriel and one of the table bouquets of lilies she'd been told to take, *since she was almost family.*

Almost family. What a concept. One that made Danita feel all warm and fuzzy inside. She'd had such a good time getting to know Maya and watching Pandora celebrate her upcoming wedding. She'd grown up dirt-poor, with very few friends. She'd worked three jobs to put herself through college, which left little time for socializing. Then she'd thrown herself wholeheartedly into her job, with little time for making friends. Today, that'd changed.

Except, it hadn't. Pandora, Maya, even Cassiopeia, they weren't real friends. This relationship was a fake. A cover. A con Gabriel was pulling on his family.

Guilt, something she'd rarely felt, overwhelmed her. It was just as well this was all fake. She'd just spent the afternoon lying to people she was wishing were friends.

So why did she suddenly wish it were real?

The friendship. The relationship. Everything between her and Gabriel.

And how was she going to convince her heart to believe it wasn't?

8

SMILING, GABRIEL LEANED back in his chair and arched a brow at the other five men at the table. None of them were looking too happy. Then again, in the last three hours playing poker, he'd won a few grand off them. He'd figured with Danita gone this afternoon, it was the perfect time to cement his spot in the good-ole-boys' club. He'd found Ham, scared up a poker game and proceeded to do what he did best. Play the game.

So far, in addition to a few grand, he'd pulled in a few enticing hints about the cartel that he figured Danita would appreciate. Nothing, though, that shed any light on who was behind it all. He figured he had another half hour, tops, before Danita returned and put an end to his little fishing expedition.

So the stakes were high. The energy was tight. His hand was crap. So it all came down to the bluff.

Just the way he liked it.

"Your bet," he reminded Ham.

The innkeeper grimaced, shifting his toothpick from one side of his mouth to the other. "You used to be more fun to play with, boy."

"I used to be seventeen," Gabriel returned with a laugh. "Who's good at that age?"

He had been. But he'd also been taught young the art of the hustle.

"Kid, you're killing me," Ham groaned, eyeing his cards before peering at Gabriel to try and gauge his hand.

"Tell ya what," Gabriel said, scooping up a tortilla chip full of guacamole and munching with a smile. "I'll give you a pass on ponying up the call money. In exchange, I win this hand, you talk me up to the boss."

"You're a sad, sad case," Mikels, the big blond goon said with a shake of his head.

"When's the head honcho gonna decide which of us is best to play leader of this band of merry criminals?" Gabriel asked, his tone as casual as a warm summer day despite having asked the same question four times already. "Doesn't he need to meet us, get a gauge on our talent in person?"

"The boss has met everyone already," Ham said, his attention on his cards. "Word will come down in due time."

"Hey now," Gabriel protested. "How'd I miss the meet and greet?"

"Quit bitchin'. The best interviews are the ones you don't realize you're having."

Shit. Gabriel forced himself to keep smiling like this new info wasn't huge. He'd already met the boss? When? Where? Before he'd come to Black Oak? Or after?

While his brain scrambled to list names of everyone he'd talked to since coming to town, his heart struggled against the knowledge that one of the people he'd talked to was his own father.

His gaze scanned the table, noting that a few of the players were as skilled as he at keeping their expression bland. A frown here, a furrowed brow there. Yeah, none of them had been aware that they'd already met the boss face-to-face, either.

"Don't think the boss is gonna care much about your pretty face and fast-talking, either," Ham said, still glaring at his cards. "A gig like this takes a lot of brains, strong connections and a serious influx of cash. I'm not much interested in your smile, Black. You want to play, you're gonna have to come up with something better."

I'm? So focused on debating his hand, Ham probably didn't realize what he'd just let slip. Gabriel did, though. Was Ham the leader of this little game? Nah. Why hide it if he was? Still, Gabriel studied the other man with narrowed eyes. Just how good was the older man at bluffing?

"He's right. You got nothing to bring to the boss," Adams said with a laugh. "We all bring a level of expertise that the boss values. Connections, merchandise. What you got? Instructions on how to look pretty? Advice on talking big?"

While the others snickered and guffawed, Gabriel's smile turned predatory. That, right there, was the key opening he'd been looking for. They were right. He would bring charm, smarts and talent to the game. But it was hard to put a value on those gifts. So he needed something more tangible.

Cash. It was damned hard to argue with a cold, hard currency. If charm wouldn't get him that top spot—and the information he needed from it—he'd go another route. He'd buy his way in.

Done with what he'd come to do, he started calculating his way out of the game.

Before he could decide whether it would be more expedient to clean them all out or to throw this hand and make Ham a happy winner, there was a clatter, the tap-a-tapping of high heels on hardwood.

"Gabriel?"

Six heads turned toward the door. Four faces glowered.

Ham looked like he wanted to declare her an angel of mercy. Gabriel just grinned.

"Hey, Blondie. I missed you."

"I see that," she said with a tiny pout and a flutter of those thick lashes. "And here I brought you back all kinds of goodies, thinking we'd have a late nap. But you're too busy playing with the boys. I guess I'll just have to take care of my afternoon cravings by myself."

Her lip jutted out just a little more, the overhead light making the glossy red pout glisten.

"They had this cake at the party, too. It's supposed to be, what do you call it? A pick-me-up? Some sort of sexual aphrodisiac, they said. I brought you back a piece. It's supposed to be really, *really* good. The cake, that is."

Gabriel had to hand it to her. Danita was pretty damned amazing with it came to acting like the ditzy tramp. A man could look at her right now, with her lashes fluttering over those sexy blue eyes and her finger trailing suggestively up her thigh and his brain had no choice but to turn to sex.

Her sigh was a work of art, the way it made those full breasts swell and her hair flutter lightly around her face. Gabriel would give her credit if he wasn't sure that little act had gotten every other guy at the table just as hard as it had him.

Jealousy was a new feeling.

And as much as he was all for experiencing new things, he couldn't say he liked it. Struggling to keep the threatening scowl from ruining his progress, Gabriel flicked his cards against the table and said, "Ham? You in or out?"

"Out," Ham said, his eyes still sliming Danita like the dirty old man he was.

"Then, gentlemen, I'm calling it a game," he said, tossing his cards toward the center of the table and scooping the pile of cash toward him. "This has been a pleasure. We'll have to play again. Higher stakes next time."

"Maybe you pony up with the girl," Yarnell smirked.

Anger blurred his vision. His hand was in a fist and he was halfway out of his chair before he realized it.

He'd never seen Danita move so fast. Not even when she was trying to scurry out of his bed. Before he could act on the violent fury pounding through him, she'd crossed the room and wrapped her arm around his waist.

Leaning into him, her breasts were warm and soft against his arm. Deciding he wanted to feel them more than he wanted to plow his fist into Yarnell's face, at least for now, he shifted to curl his own arm around Danita's shoulder.

"Sweetie pie," she breathed in a husky tone. "You promised this was going to be a fun vacation. Not all business. I'm hungry. Can we go, babe? I've got something special for you to…eat."

The last word was said in a purr as Danita traced her finger over his bottom lip. She gave the men around the table a big, airy smile. Then, making it clear she was a girl who had her priorities straight, she scooped up the pile of cash and, with it in one hand and Gabriel's wrist in the other, sauntered out of the room.

"Gentlemen," Gabriel said, tossing a smile over his shoulder. "I'll be busy this afternoon."

What the hell? His body still humming with never-before-felt jealousy, Gabriel tried to get a handle on himself. He enjoyed the show Danita's hips put on all the way up the stairs, but neither of them said a word until she'd closed the hotel room door behind them. After a quick glance at her monitoring wand on the bureau, she tossed the cash on the dresser, slapped her fists on her hips and gave Gabriel a glare.

"What the hell are you doing? I'm off gathering what little information I can at your sister's happy-ever-after party and end up with a horrible case of the guilts because your family was all so welcoming and sweet to me. I return to find you playing cards with the criminal elements, without me. We're here to gather intelligence. Not to play—or threaten—the criminals."

Gabriel leaned back against the dresser, crossing his boot-shod feet at the ankle and tucking his thumbs into his pockets. "Does this mean we're not eating cake, Blondie? Or anything tastier?"

He grinned, appreciating how good frustration looked on her as she heaved a sigh and threw her arms in the air. Was it any wonder he wanted to keep her for himself? She was simply gorgeous. The pretty blue fabric of her dress shifted, cupping her breasts before sliding down again. Gabriel's hands itched to mimic the move.

"So?" she said after sucking in another deep breath as if the air was filled with control.

"So what?"

"So you were up to something. What was the point of that game? Is there a break in the case?"

Her eyes were on his face as if she had a lie detector built into her mascara or something.

He debated for all of two seconds the option of letting her in on his little epiphany about needing to get his hands on a whole lot of cash to buy his way into the top slot of the cartel. They were here to gather information, he could hear her say. Not to make any moves.

Besides, Gabriel worked alone. And as pleasurable as this little interlude might be, he wasn't comfortable at the idea of baring his thoughts, or plans, before he knew they'd net gold.

So he offered her a shrug and his most charming smile. "I was killing time, Blondie. I figured it'd be a smart idea to spend a little time with the criminal elements. See if I could find any chinks in their armor. You know, sleuth for clues."

Still giving him that laser stare, she searched his face.

Then she tilted her head to one side and asked, "And? Did you discover anything worthwhile?"

A glib denial was on his lips. The intention to blow her off was fully formed in his mind.

But what came out of his mouth was "Maybe."

What the hell?

Gabriel grimaced, mentally cursing. What was it about her that made it impossible for him to lie to her face?

"I didn't get a break, and didn't find out who is calling the shots. But I did find out that each of these players were recruited after a year or so of pseudo-interviews. Kendall, the sheriff Caleb arrested for selling drugs a couple of months ago, was the liaison. Apparently he accessed the state database, pulled records for a number of underlings and traced them to their bosses. One of the goons, Mikels, figures each man was brought in as a specialist. No two of them have the same criminal milieu, if you will."

Danita crossed from the door and, a pretty frown furrowing her brow, dropped into the chair next to the window. Tapping her fingers on the arm of the chair, she sighed.

"That's confirmation of the intel Hunter gave us, but nothing new. Did you get anything else?"

"Apparently there are a few disgruntled rejects out there," he told her. "The goon squad was laughing about it, but Ham looked a little freaked. I guess one unhappy element stopped by the manor a few months back and tried to convince him to share the deets on who made the grave error in not hiring him instead of some of the other goons. When Ham claimed he had no clue, the guy shot up his car."

Danita sat up straighter. "Did he report it to the sheriff?"

"He said he didn't. He joked that the boss gave him a new ride as reward for loyally keeping his trap shut." Gabriel hesitated, then decided to come clean with Danita about his suspicions. Maybe doing so would mitigate a little of the guilt over not telling her the rest of his plans. "He let something slip, though. At one point, he referred to the boss as *I*. Not *he, I*."

"Do you think he's created a fake boss to keep the heat off himself?" All traces of the breathy bimbo from earlier were gone as Danita leaned forward, intelligence and calculation clear on her face. "Is he that smart? Does he have the connections? And more importantly, does he hold a grudge against your father that would lead to his trying to point his finger that way? You know him from your childhood, right? Tell me everything you remember."

Gabriel thought about it. He wasn't giving up his plan to bust the boss. But it wouldn't hurt to use FBI resources to focus on Ham while Gabriel himself made a couple of calls and nailed down the details of his bigger scam.

"There's no bad blood between him and my dad, but I don't think there's much good, either. Ham used to complain that Dad thought he was special because his ancestors founded the town. Like mine, Ham's family dates back to the origins of Black Oak. The Bollingers built the manor seventy-or-so years ago, handing down to the oldest son each generation. It used to be top-notch. A luxury destination for tourists, a fancy dinner out for locals. Since Ham's wife ditched him about fifteen years ago, he—and the manor—have been going steadily downhill. Drinking, gambling, a few bad investments. Rumor is the only reason he's held on to the manor is that it's in a trust and he can't touch it."

He watched Danita pull her phone from her purse and start tapping in information. No wonder she hadn't bothered to ruin her image and bring a laptop. Her phone clearly did the trick.

"So he has money problems? Maybe he got in over his head?" she asked, glancing up.

"Ham is good at the image of a stand-up guy, and I'm betting most of the town still buys it. Hell, even my aunt does and she's not one for tolerating bullshit."

"I spent a lot of time with your aunt today. She doesn't seem the type to tolerate someone in her circle who's even rumored to have a drinking or gambling problem."

"Yep, you're right. But he's still there. She even mentioned the other night that she's tapping him for her upcoming campaign for state representative."

"Ham's helping your aunt?"

Ham was key, but Gabriel couldn't bring himself to care much. He'd much rather focus on Danita. On the way her soft blond hair curved over her cheek as she searched for info on that little phone. The intelligence in her eyes was as erotic as the curve of her naked breasts had been. Damn, he had it bad.

"Gabriel?" she prompted.

Pulling his focus back, he just shrugged. "He was on her mayoral campaign committee. She's big on recycling, so she probably just called together the same people to run things this time."

"I'll have to check to see who else is on the committee," she said, tapping a note into her phone.

"You're so damned beautiful," Gabriel said, murmuring his thoughts aloud without realizing it. He gave an infinitesimal grimace, then mentally shrugged. Facts were facts; she was obviously gorgeous.

Just as obvious was the confused doubt in those big blue eyes.

"What're you playing at?" she asked, leaning back in the chair as if she could distance herself from whatever net he was tossing her way.

"No game," he said with a grin, realizing it was the pure truth. Something he rarely explored, let alone shared aloud.

"I'm just realizing that the more time we spend together, the more I don't know about you. And the more I want to."

She wet her lips, the nervous gesture matching the look in her eyes. "We're here to do a job. You have all the information necessary for that. There's nothing else you need to know."

But there was.

Like the light shining bright through the gray clouds and sparkling into the room, the more he saw of Danita, the more entranced he was. And the more he wanted to know.

The more he needed to understand.

And the more nervous that made her.

Gabriel had a gift for knowing the right time to play his hand. And this moment, he knew as his eyes skimmed over her face, wasn't the right one.

He was a man used to biding his time. He didn't mind waiting.

Because he knew, in his heart, when he made the move... Danita was going to be his.

DANITA HAD ONCE BEEN held at gunpoint by an obsessive woman who thought she'd slept with her husband. Given that Danita had been caught in the man's bedroom, wearing a tiny silk nighty and rockin' heels and a hidden wire, the woman had had good reason for her accusation.

That hadn't made the very real concern Danita had felt that her career—and her life—were about finished from terrifying her.

Yet that apprehension had been nothing compared to how she was feeling right this second.

Gabriel had no weapon, other than that wicked smile and a boatload of charm. She wasn't trapped, other than by virtue of having to finish the job she'd been sent here to do. And she wasn't vulnerable.

She pulled her gaze away from the man lounging on the bed, feet crossed at the ankles and his hands crossed behind his head in complete ease.

She shouldn't be vulnerable, dammit. Just because she'd slept with him, just because he made her feel things, want things she'd never imagined?

She'd rather face down the jealous harpy with the gun.

She jumped, almost sending her phone flying across the room in surprise when Gabriel leapt to his feet.

"C'mon," he said, grabbing her hand. "Get your purse, let's go."

"Where?" she asked, barely snagging the straps of her bag as he pulled her to the door. "Did you remember something? A break?"

"Exactly," he muttered, opening the door. Before she could step through, though, he spun toward her and, before she could blink, had his hands tunneled in her hair and his mouth devouring hers.

Danita's body melted.

"If you do that on this side of the door, I'm coming back with a video camera, Black," a voice mocked, growing distant as whomever it was passed them in the hall.

So lost in his mouth and the deliciously wild sensations it was stirring in her body, she doubted she'd care if whoever that was returned with an entire camera crew. All she cared about, all she could think about, was how Gabriel made her feel. About the wonderful warmth flooding her body. God, he was amazing.

Then, as the budding videographer gave a crude laugh, Gabriel slowly, gently pulled away. Danita wasn't ready, though. Her lips ached, her body pressed tight against his hoping to tempt him to kiss her again.

"Cover," Gabriel breathed against her lips as he brushed his mouth over hers softly before pulling away.

"Um, yeah. Right," she babbled, trying to jump-start her brain again. But all she could think about was the taste of him. The power of that kiss.

Like a key unlocking the secret corner of her mind, that corner she'd shoved last night's lovemaking into, the power and emotions of that event flooded her.

She barely noticed Gabriel's hand leading her downstairs. Didn't blink when he opened the passenger door to her car and bundled her into the leather seat.

By the time he'd come around the car and slid into the driver's seat, she'd caught her breath. But it wasn't until he'd started the engine that the big block's rumble shook her brains back into place.

"Where are we going?" she asked, reaching into her purse for the protection of sunglasses before looking at him. "Do you have a break in the case?"

"Nope."

It was hard to keep the flames of passion burning on High when they were being doused with waves of frustration.

"So where are we going?" she asked again, this time through clenched teeth.

"Road trip." He glanced over with a boyish smile. "I figured we needed a break. This is a gorgeous part of the state, have you ever been through the Santa Cruz Mountains before?"

It was five miles before she managed to pull her jaw off her chest.

"We're going on a joyride?" she finally said, turning in the seat and angling her body toward him as if she had a shot at intimidation. "We're on a job, Black. A job that, if not done correctly, will result in your father's arrest. And your answer is to take a scenic drive?"

"Sure. Why not?"

She'd scream, but she had the feeling she was going to need every breath she had to win this argument.

"Why not? Because it's irresponsible. That's why not. Because it's wasting precious time. Because—"

"Because we need a break. Because this afternoon was intense for both of us and we'll perform better, and think clearer, after a brief hiatus from playing cops and robbers."

As his laughter washed over her, Danita considered protesting. But the image of the tarot cards flashed in her mind. As much as The Lovers card had freaked her out, it was the undefined Death card that worried her. Because she didn't know if it applied to her, or the lover she'd taken.

Or which scared her more.

"Fine," she finally agreed. "But we're only taking a short break. Then we get right back to work."

Gabriel's laugh was infectious, like a naughty little boy found with his hand in the cookie jar. Caught, but not repentant.

"You know what?" he said. "You're going to make a great mother someday. You have that stern authoritarian thing going on. Throw in that nurturing instinct you try to hide, the sweet smile that would make anyone do anything to make you happy? Yeah, you'd be scoring a mom of the year mug on a regular basis."

Well, that shut her up. Danita's lower lip trembled for a second before she gathered enough control to tear her gaze away from Gabriel.

Her? A good mother? That was crazy. She was a federal agent, she risked her life for a living. Well, maybe not so much risked it, but the potential was always there. He knew that, and he still thought she'd be a good mom?

Had he meant it? He hadn't sounded sarcastic, that'd been genuine amusement in his tone.

Of course, he didn't know her. Not really.

He didn't know her past. The squalid despair she'd grown up in. The horrible parental examples she had to follow.

She figured if he knew that side of her, he'd be suggesting sterilization options.

Still, she couldn't rid herself of the tiny thrill that he'd think that of her.

Four hours later, that thrill was still alive and well, burning bright in her heart.

"You're wrong. Aerosmith does 'Mama Kin' much better than Guns N' Roses," she argued, poking her forkful of apple pie toward Gabriel for emphasis.

"You ever see them in concert? Aerosmith, I mean."

"Five years ago," she admitted with a smile, remembering the thrill of the music pounding, the crowd screaming and the robot dancing on stage. "You?"

Enjoying so much more than the pie, Danita grinned. For the rest of their dessert, they continued to discuss bands, books and pop culture. Flushing a little, she leaned forward to admit, "When I first started in law enforcement, I used to work as a security for hire."

Gabriel arched his brows over eyes dancing with amused anticipation. "And?"

"I escorted New Kids on the Block," she said, whispering as if she were disclosing a dirty secret. "To and from their hotel for a show they did in D.C."

Gabriel looked as worried as if she'd admitted she was a pole dancer on weekends. "And?" he prodded, obviously figuring there was more to her story than just the job.

"And," she said slowly, pressing the back of her fork into the pie crust flakes on her plate, "they were such nice guys, I ended up buying their CD."

"Oh, Danita." He shook his head in mock disappointment. But his lips twitched. And there was something in his eyes that made her squint.

"You owned that CD, didn't you?" she challenged.

"No way."

Danita rounded her eyes insistently, making Gabriel laugh again. "Okay, okay. But I didn't have the CD. I did, however, take a date to see them in concert once. Her choice, not mine," he defended.

"And you liked them," she realized, giggling as she laid her hand over the back of his in sympathetic camaraderie for the fall of another hard-core rock fan.

Before she realized she'd made a first move like that, Gabriel had turned his hand over so they were palm to palm, and linked his fingers with hers. Her heart gave a tiny sigh at the sweetness of it. Her stomach clenched at how right it felt.

"So," she said, casting her mind around for a safe subject to switch to. Discussing the job had been tacitly off-limits for the last few hours. Maybe it was time to get back to work.

But before she could bring up any thoughts about Ham or the goon squad, Gabriel lifted their joined hands and brushed a soft kiss over the back of hers.

"This was nice," he said, his words quiet but still easy to hear over the clashing dishes and loud voices in the diner. "I had a fun afternoon. I can't say that very often. Fun isn't usually on my agenda."

"Mine either," she admitted.

"Not even as a kid?"

"Survival was my agenda as a kid," she said before she thought to temper her honesty. "I guess that carried into my adult life, too. I've spent more time looking for stability than for fun."

After the words were out, she winced, sure Gabriel was going to poke and dig into her past. She lifted her chin, ready to defend her vulnerabilities. But instead he tossed a twenty on the table to cover their pie and coffee and gestured toward the door. "Ready to go?"

"Sure." Her brow furrowed, she took his hand and slid from the booth. Together they left the diner. Once settled in the car, he gave her a smile that made that spot between her shoulder blades—the one that warned her of trouble—itch.

"Given the rumors you might have heard about my father, you'd probably imagine we grew up with a lot of instability too," he said. She grinned over his careful tap dance around legalities. "But that's one thing I have to admire. He did everything he could to give us a solid foundation. We grew up in the house he bought when he married Mom. He made us go to school, made us learn the value of the day-to-day. We traveled the world. We met heads of state, movie stars, millionaires. None of whom would recognize us ever again, of course," he said with a laugh, his delight at his upbringing clear on his face. "Even while he taught us the finer points in, well, let's just say getting ahead."

"Wasn't that hard, though? I mean, did it fill you with a desire for normalcy because you had that half the time? Or did it fuel your need for a more exciting life because of your exposure to your father's, um, hobbies?"

Gabriel's grin widened as he started the car.

"Oh, I definitely want the excitement. But I didn't realize until coming home, until seeing my family through your eyes, how much I missed the rest of it."

"Normalcy?"

"How about we call it family instead." He shot her a look. "Sometimes we can leave behind the parts we don't like. The stuff that doesn't suit us. But we can still look back with pride at the stuff that worked. I'll bet you had a lot that worked, even if it wasn't something you want to revisit."

What the hell was she supposed to do when the one person who seemed to understand her inside and out—and appreciate her all the more because of that understanding—was a known criminal under her protective custody?

One who, she was pretty sure, was still pulling multiple levels of cons on everyone he knew. Including her.

9

EVER SINCE THEIR friendly drive and chat over pie three days before, Danita had been careful to keep her shields in place and Gabriel at arm's length. Irritated, he watched her across Cassiopeia's living room, trying to figure out why it was bothering him so much.

"You look like a man whose suffering a deep well of frustration."

Sighing, Gabriel turned to face the other thing that was bothering him. "Nope. I'm fine, Dad."

"Used to be, you came to me when you had a problem. You liked to bounce ideas, talk things through while you figured them out."

"Used to be's are a long time ago," Gabriel said with a shrug. "You made your choices. I made mine. Funny thing about choices, once they're made, there's no going back to used to be."

After a contemplative look, Tobias gave a slow nod. His dark hair was tidy, his sport jacket dressing up jeans for another of Cassiopeia's parties, this time a pre-wedding meet-and-greet with Pandora's family. But the look in his eyes was shrewd and amused. Like he saw right through whatever games Gabriel was playing and was just waiting to see if his son could handle it. Or not.

Gabriel had grown up with that look.

It had been how his father had taught his children. Some would say by giving them just enough rope to hang themselves. In the Black family, though, it was more a matter of giving them just enough leeway to see if they could fly.

And always, always being there to catch them if they fell.

Until he hadn't been.

"You've got your hands full, son. The trick to juggling well is to make sure the balls you value most are the ones you keep closest."

Gabriel grinned. "And here I thought you'd say the trick is to not juggle anything you don't want to break."

"Sometimes we have to risk what we value most. That's the only way we know if we're worthy of it."

Gabriel's gaze cut across the room to Danita, who was laughing with Maya and Pandora. Her blond hair was straight tonight, falling in a silken curtain to her chin and framing her lovely face. Was he worthy? Did it matter? He was the complete opposite of everything she stood for. That took him a step beyond unworthy, he figured.

"And when we realize that worthy isn't enough?" he asked, unable to help himself.

"Then we figure out a way to step up the game. If the prize is worth having, it's worth busting your ass for." Tobias's sigh pulled Gabriel's attention away from Danita. He noted signs of stress, sleepless nights and worry on his father's face. Age? Or did Tobias have a clue that he was under investigation? Hunter had indicated the master con was either behind the crime ring, or behind the eight ball.

Though Gabriel had claimed his father's innocence, he hadn't really cared. If he'd found out Tobias was the goon squad's boss, he'd have found a way to twist the finger to point it elsewhere.

But the evidence of his father's innocence was there, in the dark circles under his blue eyes, in the grooves furrowed in his brow. No con ever put signs of wear on Tobias Black. Worry did.

"Dad?" he started, not sure what, exactly, he was going to say.

He hated to admit, even to himself, how grateful he was when his cell phone buzzed in his pocket.

"Excuse me," he said, reaching for the phone, willing to take even a telemarketer call to get out of this conversation. "I've got to take this."

It took a single glance at the screen for his heart to race. Keeping it casual, he wove through furniture shaped like body parts and pedestals holding crystal balls, toward the front door without looking like he was in a hurry. A smile here, a wave there let him avoid friendly faces. He pressed Talk at the same time he walked out the front door of Cassiopeia's house.

"Hey there, Colby," he greeted as he stepped out onto the sidewalk in the chilly night. "I wasn't sure you were going to call me back."

"I debated for a bit, but then I decided it'd be rude to leave you hanging." The response was amused and easy.

"And you're never rude," Gabriel agreed with a laugh.

Which he'd hoped would factor in. But given the favor he was asking, he hadn't counted on it. He and Colby went way back. Both sons of notorious, and unprosecuted, criminal factions. But while Gabriel had embraced Tobias's legacy, Colby had turned his back on his, distancing himself from the talents of the late Antony Grayson's talent as a master counterfeiter.

It was a testament to how desperate he was that Gabriel

was willing to risk their friendship and ask him to close that distance.

"How're you doing, Gabriel? Taking a break in Black Oak or are you thinking of settling back into the arms of the family?"

"Just a break. And if you know I'm here, you probably know the details of why?"

"I couldn't garner much info on the hot blonde, but I have a pretty clear picture of what you're dealing with."

Yet another nice thing about dealing with Colby. The man did his homework and had one hell of a brain. If he'd ever turned his talent to cons, Gabriel would have had major competition. But no, his old friend had gone the crazy route and joined the military instead.

"I need a stake," Gabriel said, getting straight to the point. "A traceable, convictable stake. A couple hundred K or thereabouts. Enough to get me an introduction to whoever's calling the shots here, and guarantee they go down once I know where to shine the legal lights."

The silence was long enough to make the skin between Gabriel's shoulder blades itch. Finally, he heard the clink of ice hitting a glass, then a long sigh.

"You're asking a lot, buddy. You know I'm no artist."

"I'm not asking you to manufacture anything. Just to donate a little of the artwork your father left behind for my project."

"My father's style is distinctive. What guarantee do I have that this won't come back and kick my ass?"

"Your glowing reputation." Gabriel waited until Colby'd finished laughing before adding, "And my promise."

The laughter faded. The tension in Gabriel's shoulders, combined with the cold February night air, made him feel like he was about to shatter.

Finally, "Fine, but you'll owe me. I'll have it delivered to you by this time tomorrow."

"I appreciate it," Gabriel said, relief rushing through him. It was a good plan, and the counterfeit money was vital to pulling it off. But still, he was asking one hell of a lot from his old pal.

"In exchange, you tell me the whole story," Colby said in his smooth, easy tone. "And introduce me to the blonde."

"The story's yours," Gabriel agreed with a laugh. "But the blonde is mine."

"So that's how it is?"

Staring across the lawn with its collection of naked statuary, twinkling heart-shaped lights and bare-root roses, Gabriel sighed. He had a hell of a lot more confidence in pulling off this scam than he did in making his relationship with Danita a reality.

Still…

"Yeah," he said, falling back on the art of believing that if you said the lie often enough, it'd become reality. "That is exactly how it is."

Colby's laugh had the wicked edge of a man who'd never fallen off that scary emotional cliff.

"Twenty-four hours," he said, still guffawing as he hung up.

One day. Then he'd bluff his way through the biggest game he'd ever played.

Great. Nothing more fun than bluffing with a bunch of guys who liked to shoot their opponents. He didn't know if it was the stakes, or the game itself, but he was getting tired of playing. For the first time in his life, Gabriel considered the option of this being his last game. After all, would he ever play for higher stakes? Damned hard to top this.

"Gabriel?"

Tucking his phone in his pocket, he turned toward Danita.

"Your father said you'd come out here. What's up?" she asked, her gaze sliding toward his pocket, then meeting his again.

"Just taking a call."

She tilted her head to one side, giving him that searching look again. The woman was scary, the way she made him feel like she could see straight through to his soul.

"Is it getting to be too much?" she asked quietly, slowly walking toward him and stopping a few inches away so their conversation stayed private.

He breathed in the wildflower scent of her, letting it warm him with the memory of her body, naked and wild, poised over his. This distance thing of hers was driving him crazy.

Then again, didn't he specialize in keeping people at a distance?

"Gabriel?" she asked quietly, her face concerned, the hand on his arm warm and comforting.

Maybe, just maybe, it was time to quit shoving people—certain select people—away.

"Let's go," he said, giving her a quick look. She didn't have her coat. But she wore a tiny glittery purse like an accessory, the long strap crossed between her breasts. She'd have her gun, whatever toys mattered to her, there in that bag. Good enough. He took her hand and headed toward the Corvette.

"What's the deal?" she asked, giving him a baffled look as she hurried to keep up in her high heels.

"We have business to take care of," he decided.

"What business? Where?" She threw a quick look over her shoulder toward the Cassiopeia's, with its crowd of family and out-of-town friends who'd arrived for the wedding in three days. "Shouldn't we say something to your family? Let them know we're leaving?"

"They'll figure it out," he said, bundling her into the passenger seat and striding around the car as fast as he could.

He had twenty-four hours before this game shifted into high gear. One way or another, things were getting scary tomorrow. So tonight? Tonight he was living out his dreams.

And all of them involved Danita being naked.

DANITA DIDN'T KNOW what was bothering Gabriel, but she knew it was major. She'd watched him play the goon squad like a master cellist played his instrument. His family tended to get him on edge, but more in a melancholy sort of way.

But this wasn't melancholy. This, she decided as she surveyed his face with a worried frown, this was bigger. Whatever was bothering Gabriel was bigger. Desperate. Personal.

She sat, silent, while he drove, letting him wrestle with whatever it was. After about ten minutes on a dark road, he turned off into a weedy clearing. The pitted dirt road played hell on her 'Vette's suspension, making her wince.

"Where are we?" she asked, looking around in a combination of curiosity and concern. There was a barn ahead, but there were no animals around. No crops, either. The red siding looked flaked and droopy in the moonlight, while there was little white left on the trim.

"My favorite hideaway when I lived in Black Oak," Gabriel told her, leaning one arm over the steering wheel while he stared nostalgically at the decrepit building. "I used to come here and hatch plots."

"And bring girls?"

His eyes cut to hers, amusement dancing in the gold depths. "Of course."

He snagged the keys from the ignition and tilted his head. "Care to take a trip down memory lane with me?"

She should say no. She'd been so careful to keep a tidy professional distance between them over the last few days. But she couldn't resist a chance to see where Gabriel had honed his talent...so to speak.

Before the second—smarter—thoughts could set in, Gabriel was there opening her door and offering a hand to assist her from the car.

"C'mon," he said, shrugging off his coat and wrapping it around her shoulders. "I wonder if it's changed much."

She wrinkled her nose as they stepped through the knee-high weeds, grateful she'd worn boots tonight instead of sandals. "It looks like it's sat abandoned since you left."

"A shame," he said, one hand wrapped tight around hers. The door squealed in protest as he pushed it open. He reached a familiar hand around and flipped a switch, but they were both surprised when the weak yellow light lit overhead. "It was a great hideaway. It'd be a bummer if no other teenage boy discovered the pleasures to be had here."

"You mean girls to be had?"

"Same thing," he agreed, his smile flashing as he looked around. "You know, for being a dive on the outside, it's still in pretty good shape in here."

The dirt floor was, well, dirty, with scuffed footsteps in here and there among the hay that had scattered out of the stacked bales. A long workbench spanned one wall, one wooden leg shattered so it all listed to one side. Bales of yellowing hay scented the space with fresh, country appeal and there was a loft running along one end, but no apparent ladder to access the space.

"This is fresh hay," she said, poking a finger at the sweet-smelling grassy piles. "I guess your old haunt isn't so abandoned after all."

"Fancy that," he said absently.

Danita glanced over, wondering what had him distracted. The past, she realized when she saw the bittersweet smile on his face. Her heart melted a little when he traced his finger over initials carved in the graying splintered wood of one wallboard.

"*GB? No luvs 4ever?*" she teased, wondering if he'd been such a player even as a teen that he'd known not to make a public—or in this case, barn—commitment.

"I didn't write it." He laughed. She looked closer, seeing the loopiness of the letters and what looked like raindrops next to the heart.

"Those are teardrops?" she realized. "Were you already breaking hearts back then?"

"I never made a promise I couldn't keep," he said in a self-righteous tone that was ruined by his reminiscent grin, pure triumphant male.

He was so damned cute, she thought as she settled onto a surprisingly clean bale of hay. Cute and sweet.

"So this really was your love nest," she mused. "Are there notches somewhere?"

"Blondie, I might have brought a lot of girls here, but none of them could hold a candle to you."

"Uh-huh," she said, giving him an arch look. "Not even Kathy?"

Gabriel's smile didn't dim. If anything, it widened in delight. "Ahh, Kathy Andrews," he reminisced. "One fine summer night, a six-pack of wine coolers and a pretty blonde. The stuff great memories are made of."

"We chatted at the bridal shower," Danita said with a laugh. "She remembers you fondly, too. She mentioned a spring fling, setting the bar high and crème de menthe liqueur."

Danita watched Gabriel laugh. A week was such a short time to spend with someone. Most people would scoff at the idea that two people could connect, could really understand each other that quickly. But in her business, and she imagined in Gabriel's too, they had to make snap judgments, to understand people quickly.

And she understood him.

He was a clever man, and one who was determined to win at all costs. But he was, in his own way, an honest man with a code of conduct he wouldn't budge from. The fact that, after their first night together, he'd insisted on taking the sleeping bag so she could have the bed, told her so much. He'd respected her boundaries and he hadn't made her feel stupid for needing them.

He'd brought her into his family, a family who'd embraced and welcomed her like her own never had.

He made her feel…whole. When she hadn't ever been able to admit, even to herself, that she was fractured.

So a week wasn't long. Nor were the few days they had left. But she was a smart woman. And smart women didn't waste precious time.

Before she could talk herself out of it, she rose from the softly scented hay to cross the dirt floor. Stopping just inches from Gabriel, she hesitated. Then, swallowing hard to wet her dry throat, she reached out to rub her hands over his arms, covered only in a thin sweater.

"What's up?" he asked quietly, the laughter fading as his eyes locked on hers.

"You took on a lot," she said quietly as she studied his face. "Coming home. Facing your past, risking your reputation. Deceiving your family while they are in danger. We didn't, or at least I didn't, consider how hard this would be for you."

"There's a lot at stake," he said slowly, frowning as he stared back at her as if trying to figure out her game.

Her lips twitched. That was Gabriel, always looking for the con. She wasn't sure if he realized his hands had tangled in her hair, the move was so automatic now.

"My father, and by extension my family, is in danger. True, you didn't give me much choice about coming home. I wouldn't have known about it if not for you, though. So while your method, other than that kiss the night you arrested me, sucked a little... I guess I'm glad you did it."

Danita's smile shifted from sympathetic to naughty. She leaned closer to brush a quick kiss over his cheek, then arched one brow. "So you're thanking me for arresting you?"

"Um, no." His grimace was little-boy cute. "And given that you're the first arrest I've ever had, and it's going down as solicitation, I think you owe me for messing with my rep."

Just the opening she was looking for. Danita inched closer so her breasts skimmed his chest as she slid her hands up to the hard breadth of his shoulders. "Then I should make that up to you, shouldn't I?"

"I was kidding. I didn't bring you here for seduction," he said, his words as serious as a vow.

"I know." She smiled up at him, her heart telling her this was the right decision. "Which makes me seducing you that much more fun."

"You're going to seduce me?" His smile was as wicked as the hands curving over her ass. In typical Gabriel fashion, he didn't pretend to hesitate, but instead dove right in for the fun.

"I am. And I'm going to do a damned good job of it, too," she promised. Figuring there was no time like the present to start, she angled her body tighter to his. Running her fingers through the silky thickness of his hair and she gave him a slow, suggestive smile. "So good, you'll never forget tonight."

In her heels, she barely had to stretch to brush her lips gently over the soft warmth of his. She breathed in his scent, so familiar after practically living with him for almost a week. The hard planes of his chest pressed against her, cushioned slightly by the light wool of the sport coat he'd wrapped around her earlier.

"Babe, I don't plan on forgetting one single thing about you." With one last squeeze of appreciation, his hands moved from her butt to the indention of her waist. Her skin tingled with heat, even through the layers of fabric.

He'd never forget her? Line or truth? Did it matter? Danita told herself it didn't, even as her heart tucked the words away like a precious gift.

"So tell me," she asked quietly. "What's your secret fantasy? What kind of sex makes you melt? We've already done it hot and fast. We've played on the edges of kink. Do you like it a little nasty? What's your pleasure, Gabriel Black?"

Amusement faded. His hands tightened on her waist, then slid around her back, pulling her closer, tighter against his already hardening body.

"My pleasure? You, Danita," he said quietly. A thrill shimmered in her heart at the sound of her name on his lips. "I want you, the way you want to be wanted."

Amused, she shook her head, even as she gave in to the unspoken invitation to heat things up and skimmed her fingers down his chest. Her nails lightly scraped over his nipples, making them harden through his thin sweater.

"My fantasy is your fantasy? Isn't that a bit of a cop-out? What's the deal, Gabriel? You don't think I can handle your idea of the best sex you can imagine?"

He cupped her breasts in his hands now, gently squeezing the mounds in an erotic rhythm. "Babe, I promise. There's nothing that will get me hotter than knowing you're living out your fantasy with me. There's nothing more exciting than knowing that I'm the man who makes you crazy with wanting. You have your way with me, and I promise, it'll be the best sex I've ever had in my life."

Danita blinked away the sudden tears that blurred her view of his gorgeous face.

"Undress me," she ordered softly, finally taking him at his word. "Undress me like I'm the most precious thing in your world."

And he did. His mouth skimming over hers, he pushed the jacket from her shoulders, then shifted to pull her purse over her head. His mouth followed the line of his fingers as he slipped each tiny button of her blouse open. His breath was warm, his fingers tender as he slipped the ruffled chiffon fabric off her shoulders.

His kisses were sweet, but still hot enough to send shivers of pleasure through every erogenous zone she had. He took her aching nipple into his mouth, suckling and sipping in a sweet, adoring way that made her head spin. He quickly unbuttoned her skirt, his hands leaving a trail of warmth vivid in the chilly barn as he pushed the fabric off her hips.

Then, making her mewl in protest, he released her breast and stood back to give her an inspection that was just as hot as his caress.

Standing in her stockings, a scrap of lace and boots, Danita waited. Nerves danced. Before they could take hold, though, she saw the look in his eyes. Hot appreciation, a healthy dose of lust and something else. Something that made her heart melt.

Adoration.

Oh, God, she realized as her breath tangled in her chest. She was in so much trouble. She was so in love with him.

She'd never planned on falling in love. Given her history, she wasn't even sure she believed in it. But now? Given that her feelings for Gabriel poured through her like molten lava, burning through every part of her being, she had to believe.

Her heart raced, terror at the depth of her feelings chasing the warmth. To distract herself from letting the realization completely freak her out, she stepped into the warmth of Gabriel's waiting arms, wrapped one leg around his thigh and pressed her mouth to his.

Clearly appreciating the access, his fingers curled around

her thigh, hitching her leg higher before sliding over her wet folds. Danita almost lost her balance, it felt so intense.

"C'mere," he said, releasing her mouth. With a quick glance around, he pulled her over to a bale of hay. He squinted at it, then at her and shook his head. "Can't scratch your sweet flesh."

With that and a quick shove, he'd dropped his pants. He had the condom on and her straddling his lap before she could kick off her shoes. She was sure she'd never wear boots again without thinking of Gabriel.

He impaled her. The hard, throbbing length of him slid into her welcoming heat in a single smooth, easy thrust.

Danita leaned back, trusting Gabriel's hands at her waist to keep her from falling as she rode his body. Her ankles anchored behind his waist, it was like free-falling in delight.

Within seconds, the passion enveloped her. The climax started gently, a slow ripple. Then it tightened. Her breath came in pants as she grabbed on to the promise that pleasure offered, suddenly desperate to complete the ride.

His fingers dug into the soft flesh of her hips, keeping her body moving to his rhythm. Feeling her body tighten, he released one hip to tease his fingers over her thighs, reach between their bodies and tweak her throbbing, wet clitoris.

That's all her body needed to send it flying to pieces. Crying out, she barely realized he'd shifted his hand to the small of her back to keep her from falling backward as he thrust his way to his own explosion.

Still spinning with delight, they collapsed into each other, both trying to catch their breath. The damp flesh of her thighs still trembled as she unlocked her feet from behind his waist and let them fall to the dirt floor.

It was another minute—or a few days, she could barely tell—before Danita could lift her head off Gabriel's shoulder.

"Wow," he breathed. "You do that fantasy thing really, really well."

Pleasure filled her, making Danita even warmer than that red-hot orgasm had. She pressed a soft kiss against his cheek before standing.

"You okay?" she asked, pressing her lips tight to hold back the giggle at the sight of him hobbling to his own feet. Had she broke something important in that ride?

"There's a distinct possibility that I have hay burns on my ass," he said with an amused grimace as he stood and rubbed one hand over his bare butt. "But it was definitely worth it."

Laughing, Danita reached out a hand to pull Gabriel to his feet. "Thank you for playing Prince Charming and saving me from the rough hay."

"It was rougher than I remember," he said with a grin, pulling his boxers and slacks up. "Toward the end there, I felt like I had a pitchfork poking me in the back. It added an interesting urgency to the fun."

"Baby," she teased.

Then the hay rustled. There was a crash, metal against metal, echoing like a shot through the decrepit old barn. Danita's eyes rounded and her hand flew to her hip. Her naked hip. Where was her gun? Damn, what a time to be naked.

"What the…"

Instead of panicking, Gabriel simply hooked his slacks and stepped toward the dark end of the barn. Scrambling into her clothes as fast as she could find them, Danita hissed for him to wait. He waved a hand at her to chill. Concern for him poured through her. A warning was on the top of her tongue, but before she could spit it out, there was another crash.

Then a tiny, sad meow.

"A cat?" she said, her fingers pausing as she tried to find the hook of her skirt. "It's just a cat?"

She almost dropped to the dirt floor in relief. The meow came again, this time a little closer. Peering into the darker end of the barn, she and Gabriel both called out, "Kitty? Here, kitty kitty."

There was a rustling. Then sudden movement on the bale of hay next to their personal love nest.

"Ohh," Danita breathed, her heart melting at the sight of the gorgeous cat. Maybe a year or two old, it was a wide-eyed calico with a darling face. Meowing louder, it padded toward them slowly, as if it were willing to give them a chance but ready to run at any second.

"Isn't it sweet?" she said, keeping her voice soft as she stepped closer and knelt a few feet away from the cat. Slowly, carefully, Danita reached out one hand and made a soft tutting sound, rubbing her fingers together to get the kitty's attention. "She's beautiful, isn't she?"

Slowly, her eyes darting back and forth between the two humans, the cat padded forward until she was inches away from Danita's fingers. She paused. Danita was careful not to move. Then with a growly sort of meow, the cat butted her head against Danita's outstretched hand.

Taking that as an okay, she gathered the kitty in her arms.

"I always wanted a cat growing up," she told the calico, smiling into its mottled face and rubbing her index finger over the black spot on its nose. "We couldn't though. Too much trouble, too expensive. But you're not trouble, are you?"

Her blouse lying forgotten on the ground, Danita sighed with joy. The cat purring in her arms, she looked up to see Gabriel giving her an indecipherable look. There was a sweetness in his smile that made her heart speed up and her breath catch.

"What?" she asked.

"Looks like you've found a friend."

Danita's smile fell.

"She feels so thin but she's too friendly to be feral. A stray, maybe?" she said quietly. "This barn is too far out for her to live nearby."

Thinking of leaving the cat here, alone, broke her heart. But it would totally ridiculous to take it with them. She was on a case. Staying at a hotel. Even if she did, she wasn't in any position to take care of a pet. Not with her job.

She looked into the pale green eyes and sighed. But oh, man, did she want to.

"What are we going to do with her?" she asked quietly.

"Take her home with us, of course."

Staring up at him as Gabriel took the cat into his own arms and gestured for her to get dressed, she slowly rose. He rubbed a knuckle along the furry ears, talking soothing nonsense to keep the feline calm.

Shrugging into her dusty blouse, Danita slipped the buttons closed with trembling fingers and wondered how many people could pinpoint the exact moment they fell in love.

Or maybe she was just lucky, because she knew without a doubt that she'd just lost her heart to the man standing in front of her with the kitty cat.

10

WARM DREAMS, THE KIND she'd never had as a child, enveloped her in a feeling of safety and love. Danita didn't want to leave them. Except her body was demanding attention. Or, she realized as her thighs trembled with pleasure, Gabriel was demanding she pay attention to her body.

Slowly, not wanting to let go of the dream, Danita opened her eyes. The morning sun was barely a glow, it was so early. But the bed was warm, and Gabriel's body hard over hers.

"Morning," he murmured as he slid into her.

Her body, still hazy with sleep, rose on a wave of sleepy delight. Passion was gentle this morning, swirling in soft coils as Gabriel's body thrust gently. His lips were sweet against her breasts, soothing and sipping at the tips.

Then, before she could clear the sleep from her mind, her body clenched. Passion turned fiery, grabbing her in its grip and pulling her under. Her thighs convulsed around his hips, gripping tight as she flew over the edge in a climax that sent shudders powering through her in ever-widening ripples of delight.

Gabriel's thrusts grew harder, faster. His body plunged. His movements lost their usual elegant sheen and she felt him grow even harder inside her.

His growl was tight and low as he arched his back, exploding with a roar. He thrust one last time, then collapsed, his lips warm on her throat.

Danita's breathing slowed, but her pulse still raced as she smoothed her hands down his sweat-slick back.

"Well, good morning," she said in a husky whisper. "What do you say we do that again now that I'm awake?"

One hour, three orgasms and a shared shower later and Danita was sipping coffee and watching Gabriel cuddle the cat.

"I can't believe you snuck her in here," she said, trying to pretend her heart wasn't all gushy at the sight of Gabriel trying to convince the calico to eat some of the dry food in the saucer. "A cat. What are we going to do with a cat during a case?"

"Oh, please," he scoffed with a smile as the feline sniffed at the saucer of food and finally took a bite. "Like I didn't see you giving her all sorts of love last night when I got back from the store? Or coaxing her out from under the bed to sleep next to us after I fell asleep?"

"I'm not the one who drove two towns over to an all-night grocery store to get food and litter and cat toys," she said with a laugh. "I had no idea the suave and sophisticated Gabriel Black would be such a pushover for a cat."

"A pretty face is a pretty face," he mused. Then he rose from the floor to take his seat by the tiny bistro table holding coffee. "She's sweet. And scared and alone. I'm a sucker for a damsel in distress."

"What are you going to do with her when we leave?" she asked, not wanting to be a downer but knowing one of them had to be realistic. "And more to the point, while we're here?"

"I'll tell Ham today that she's in our room. He'll be chill about it. So that takes care of the now." He gave her a considering look, then shrugged. "As for later? We'll figure out custody of our baby when this is done."

"Our baby?" she choked. Custody. Like they were a couple. A couple doomed to split up. Her bubble of happiness bursting in a flash, Danita took a gulp of coffee, focusing on the hot liquid instead of the sudden pain burning in her chest.

"She needs a name, though," he said, watching the cat chow through the food so fast there were kibble bits flying across the floor. "What do you think?"

"A name?" The memory of her third-grade teacher's cat flashed. Mrs. Seton had always delighted the class with pictures, stories and one fine time the cat itself.

"Pippi," she said, even as her mind argued the insanity of this discussion and her heart warned her to get the hell out before she was in too deep. But, her glance shifted from Gabriel to the cat and back. "I like the name Pippi."

As if realizing how hard this was for her, Gabriel reached over to take her hand. He brushed a kiss over her knuckles, then winked.

"Blondie, it's all going to work out. Trust me."

Struggling, Danita finally nodded. She wondered if he knew how much she was putting on the line with that tiny jerk of her chin.

"Okay, then. I'm going to go warn Ham we're having a threesome in here now," he told her, leaning in for another kiss before giving Pippi a quick pat and heading out the door.

"I'll be here," she said quietly. Which was the problem. She shouldn't be here, waiting. She should be out working the case. Gathering information. Cozying up to the criminal elements and finding out how any of them had connections or a history with Black.

She'd lost objectivity. She didn't want the case to hurt Gabriel. So instead of following her instincts and doing exactly what needed to be done, she was wearing blinders and pretending it wasn't an issue. She wasn't running this case on logic. She was running it on emotion. And by doing so, she was putting the only thing she had, the only thing that defined her, on the line.

Her reputation as an FBI agent.

"I'm blowing it," she told Pippi. "I'm so busy playing house, I'm not working the case. I'm so worried about hurting people, I'm ignoring my job."

And in the end, the job and shared custody of a cat were all she'd have. Swallowing hard, Danita steeled her shoulders and reached for her cell phone.

Ten seconds later, "Hi, Hunter. I need some help."

THE COMBINATION bachelor and bachelorette party was a work of art. Sexual art, that was. Danita was in awe of the decorations. Cupid, or was it Eros in this case, hung from the ceiling in all his naked and well-endowed glory. His wings weren't the only thing unfurled.

Waiters made their way through the crowd with trays of tidbits, each clearly labeled with their aphrodisiac qualities. And instead of gifts, there was a large, wire-sculpture tree festooned in ribbons, each holding a wish and tidbit of bedtime advice for the happy couple. "Sexual Healing" played from the speakers.

Apparently wishing the bride and groom a fertile life together was Cassiopeia's latest party theme. Danita wondered if the happy couple wasn't wishing Tobias had let the mother of the bride pay for part of the wedding instead of going overboard on all the wild parties.

"Subtle," Gabriel said, his hand warm on her waist as he grinned at the spectacle. "It must be serious love for Caleb to put up with this."

"Would you?" she asked, laughing as she looked up at Gabriel's still slightly stunned expression. "Put up with this kind of thing? The circus of a wedding, the in-law weirdness? Everyone wishing you well and offering sex advice?"

"Well, a man can't ever rest on his sexual laurels. Learning new things keeps the love life spicy, right?" The look he gave her was pure heat. "Like last night. The things I learned about you definitely added to my sexual repertoire. I wonder if I could fit it all on one of those little strips of paper."

Danita laughed and grabbed Gabriel's arm as he moved as if to head over to the wishing tree and jot down his advice. "Stop. I'm sure your brother doesn't care about my preferences."

"No. But I do."

Her heart melted. The man was an expert at making people believe lies, but she knew when he gave her that look, his gorgeous eyes looking so sincere and his smile sweet, that he was being completely honest with her.

"You're a sweetheart, do you know that?" she asked, thrilled to see the baffled embarrassment wash over his face. "And because you are, I'm going to let you go be manly and talk to your old friends while I circulate and play the curious fiancée."

"You mean you want me to get out of your way so you can work."

Because he was smiling instead of looking offended, Danita leaned forward to give him a smacking kiss on the cheek. "Of course."

"Fine." She'd just started to turn away when his hand snagged her shoulder. "But you can do better than that."

His kiss was anything but a fun smack of the lips. Hot and silky, his lips slid over hers in sweet seduction. When he released her mouth, Danita could only blink up at him as she tried to regain her breath. What had they been talking about?

"Have fun," he said with a wink before he headed toward

the crowd surrounding Caleb. To offer all sorts of brotherly torment, she was sure.

Which would keep him happily entertained while she worked the room. Something she'd much rather do without him, since she'd been beset by minor, unfamiliar feelings of guilt for the last hour. Ever since she'd called Hunter, outlining the case so far, and Gabriel's suspicions about Ham. Suspicions she wasn't sure she believed, given all of the evidence to date. How much was a real hunch, and how much was Gabriel grasping at straws for proof of his father's innocence?

Before she could dwell on her decision, she was enveloped in a musky herbal hug and the soft silk of a vivid purple caftan.

"Danita, darling. Welcome. What do you think of our fertility festival? Isn't it a wonderful blessing for my sweet Pandora and her beau?"

Cassiopeia led Danita through the room, chatting and pointing out the party delights. Which was perfect because it let Danita scope things out under the cover of being a good guest.

Then something caught her eye. The creepy innkeeper looked like he was about to explode.

"Excuse me," she murmured to Cassiopeia with a quick, apologetic smile. Without waiting for acknowledgment, she hurried across the room.

Ham was arguing with one of the goons. A goon who, by all rights, shouldn't be here. The guy at the store's spring solstice celebration was one thing, but at a private wedding party? He'd clearly come to talk to Ham.

Or, noting the fury on his face and the worry on Ham's, to argue with the innkeeper.

Excitement surged. They knew Ham was the key. Everything she'd found on him since Gabriel pointed the finger at him assured her that if they figured out his role, they'd bust this wide-open.

She took a surreptitious step closer, wanting to hear the argument.

She caught the words *problems*, *timing* and *not enough cash yet*. She debated how she could turn this to their favor. As fast as it started, though, their argument was over. Ham looked shaken and a little ill. Trouble in paradise? She felt disloyal to Gabriel for thinking it, but she was sure Ham wasn't the ringleader. The guy clearly didn't have the personality to be a master criminal. Which left her original suspect.

Her stomach clenched in despair as she tried to decide which would suck worse. Pinning the crimes on Tobias Black, a man she'd come to like a great deal. Or the look on Gabriel's face when she arrested his father.

LATER THAT EVENING, tension draped over Gabriel's shoulders like a tight-fitting jacket. Not even watching Danita play momma to the cat had soothed his headache. Instead, it'd only added to the stress since the view made him wish for a future. One that included Danita and the cat. And, God help him, maybe even a home and commitment.

He shuddered. Before, just the thought of commitment would be enough to make him want to run like hell. Now it only made him want to search for exits, just in case.

He stood outside Ham's office door and wondered if this was the right thing to do, or if it was an exit in disguise. He hadn't told Danita what he was doing. He couldn't. He wasn't about to tiptoe along the line of the law, he was about to dance all over the wrong side. And Danita was FBI.

It didn't matter. He had to do it. Had to finish what he'd started and clear his father's name. Quickly so he couldn't change his mind, he pounded on the door.

"C'min."

The office was a mess. Clearly someone had a paper-work issue. Piles here, stacks there, the entire room reeked of desperation. Something was falling apart. The manor? Or something else? Whatever it was, Gabriel would make sure it worked to his favor.

"Ham, old buddy," he greeted with a smile filled with fake charm. "I've got a favor."

"Gabriel?" Flustered, the older man shoved one hand through his graying hair while pushing papers together on his desk with the other. His cheeks flushed, whether from the bottle of gin at his elbow or whatever he'd been doing, Gabriel didn't know. "What can I do for you?"

"The question is really what I can do for you?" Gabriel set the briefcase on the desk, but didn't open it. As expected, Ham's eyes locked on it. His brow furrowed over eyes sud-denly gleaming with greed. His fingers spasmed on the papers and he half reached for the leather case before he could stop himself.

"No," he said with a grimace. Then he shook his head and said, louder and more assured, "No. I'm already employed, Gabriel. I don't double-cross. I'm not crazy."

"Double-cross?" His tone was pure offended surprise, but only the offense was fake. "Ham, you say that like a man over his head."

The spasm wasn't so easily controlled this time as the older man gave a shudder. His eyes shot around the office, his lips white. Was the room bugged? Ham's actions, his overall air of drowning in misery, it just gave a little too much cre-dence to the idea that he was a lieutenant, not a general.

Fear that the rest of the FBI's charge might hold true as well, that his father was involved, trickled down Gabriel's spine. Refusing to let it take hold, he went into challenge mode.

"Since it's just you and me here," he snapped, "let's cut the bullshit. We both know my father has nothing to do with this gig. He's done a lot of things, but he doesn't scare people."

"You're fooling yourself if you think your daddy's lily-white, Gabriel. He's not even shades of gray."

"We both know Tobias Black's criminal days are done. What I don't know is why he's being set up to take the fall. Since it suits me to no longer have to compete with his reputation, I don't care why. What I do care about is making sure that I'm in charge of the new cartel."

"I told you, that's not an option. Everybody is equal partners, with only the boss in charge."

"The boss hasn't heard my offer yet."

"I'm not telling you who it is. I'm not making an introduction."

"But you will. Just as soon as you pass on my message," Gabriel said, patting the briefcase for emphasis, "your boss is going to be the one asking to meet with me."

Ham's eyes shifted to the bottle at his elbow with longing before he heaved a sigh. "Look, take my advice as someone whose known you most of your life and thinks you're a good guy. Get out of this. Take your charm, your girlfriend and your briefcase and head out. It's a no-win situation. Especially for you."

"Why me, especially?" Gabriel waited, tense, while Ham gave in to the shakes and swigged a quick drink of gin straight from the bottle. "Because the identity of the boss will cause me, especially, a problem?"

Ham's grimace had nothing to do with the cheapness of his drink. Gabriel's stomach clenched. Real or act? Was the guy trying to make it seem like Tobias was the boss? Or was he really worried that the boss was someone out of Gabriel's league to deal with?

He had to find out.

Dropping his friendly act, Gabriel slapped both hands on

the desk and leaned across the paper-strewn antique to glare into the other man's face.

"I'm not walking. I have a stake here. In this deal, in this town and in the direction fingers are pointing. So leaving isn't an option. Nor is sitting in the backseat."

"The front seat is already occupied," Ham said, leaning back so his chair squeaked and giving Gabriel a blurry look. "No room for anyone else."

Time to play his cards.

Gabriel straightened, laid the briefcase flat and unlatched it. Lifting the lid, he turned it so Ham could see the contents. The old guy swallowed loudly, then grabbed the bottle of gin for another swallow.

"I'm not taking bribes," he said. His words were loud and clear, cementing Gabriel's suspicion that the room was bugged.

"No bribe, my friend. This is a down payment. It's been pointed out that everyone else brought something tangible to the table. Guns, drugs, etcetera. I'm simply doing my part. I'm bringing cash."

"What makes you think we need cash? The boss is plenty loaded."

"Everybody needs cash," Gabriel said with a laugh. His hand on the table, he knew it was time to step back and let the game play out. "This is a down payment on my contribution. Fifty thousand now. A mil after I meet with your boss."

"I'll pass on the money, but that don't mean anything," Ham said, his eyes fixated on the briefcase. "Likely you won't even get a response. You're willing to pay fifty large to be ignored?"

"I'm willing to bet fifty large that I won't be." Gabriel leaned across the desk again, all semblance of friendliness gone now as his smile went scalpel-sharp. "And Ham, old buddy? If you think about double-crossing me, if you even consider taking this money for yourself and forgetting to pass it and my message on?"

Ham's Adam's apple worked as he tried to swallow.

"You do that, and you'll find out the bottom-line difference between my father and myself. He's never done anything to scare people." Gabriel paused, watching Ham's hand shake on the briefcase for a second before meeting the man's pale blue gaze. "But me? Only idiots aren't afraid of me."

Satisfied with the glaze of terror in the other man's eyes, Gabriel patted the briefcase, gave Ham a friendly nod, then turned to leave.

He didn't need one of Danita's spy devices to know that little conversation had just been transmitted, in full, to whoever's ass he was going to take down.

11

GABRIEL FIGURED HE HAD to be dreaming. But the pleasure coursing through his body was so strong, so demanding, he couldn't stay in the warm embrace of sleep. He had to climb out and see if it was real.

Shifting, his heels dug into the soft mattress as cool air wafted over his warm body. A tickling sensation swept down his chest, over his belly. Forcing his eyes open, he turned his head just in time to see Danita's mouth swallow his hard, swollen dick.

Groaning, he tangled his fingers into the silky strands of hair tickling his belly, delighting in the rhythm she set. Her tongue danced along his aching flesh, soothing before her teeth gently nipped.

His body tightened. What little blood wasn't already powering his erection drained from his brain so all Gabriel could do was feel. And damn, he felt great.

No longer a sweet gentle climb, passion clawed, demanding release. Control frayed. His body tensed as his heels dug deeper into the mattress.

"Babe," he gasped his warning, tightening his fingers to warn her to pull her head away. "C'mere."

"Nope," she said, looking up the length of his body with sultry eyes filled with feminine power. "I'm busy here."

And then she proceeded to blow Gabriel, and every shred of his control. Sucking hard on the sensitive head of his dick, her tongue swirled. Her mouth slid up, then down, then up again before she sucked again. Gabriel's fingers tightened again, trying to pull her back. He wanted more. Wanted to taste her, to pour himself into her.

But she wouldn't budge. Instead she sucked harder.

And Gabriel exploded. Lights flashed behind his eyes. A groan ripped from his throat. Danita gave a hum filled with power and delight as she swallowed.

Gabriel didn't know if he should be surprised or embarrassed that he was shaking. Had any woman ever had this much power over him? Had he ever wanted a woman this much?

He tried to reel in his brain cells, but Danita chose that moment to slide her way up his body.

"Yum," she said when she reached his mouth. She gave him a warm kiss before snuggling, her face buried in the curve of his throat and her delicious body pressed tight against his. "Now that's what I call my early-morning wake-up call."

"That's what I call fabulous," he said, his heart still racing. He ran a hand up the silky smooth side of her body until he reached the heavy weight of her breast, resting on his chest. Curving his palm over the hardened tip, he pressed a kiss against the top of her head. "Its turnaround time, babe."

"Oh, please," she said, tilting her head back to give him a wide, wicked smile. "I took you down."

"And did a damned good job of it, too," he said with a grin that oozed with satisfaction. Then, with a sudden, guilty start, he looked around the room. "Um, where's Pippi? I don't want to damage her psyche or anything."

"Aren't you cute?" Danita laughed, leaning in to give him the sweetest of kisses. "She was scratching at the window this morning so I let her out to roam."

"Then we're alone?" He grinned again. "Then let's see how fast I can get back in the game."

Fast was an understatement. He'd had her on her back, ankles draped over his shoulders while she screamed satisfaction within twenty minutes.

And two hours later, Gabriel's grin had shifted to cocky. He figured he had a right, though. Waking to fabulous sex, then watching Danita fly apart under his mouth not twice, but three incredible times. Yeah, he had all rights to cocky.

"C'mon," he hurried her again. This time it was with eggs and bacon in mind, though. "Pippi's napping off her disappointment after her failed morning bird hunt and I want to get to the diner while the biscuits are fresh. A morning filled with hot, wild sex has me starving."

"I've noticed that you're always starving in the morning," she said, checking her gun, then tucking it into her purse before she gave him a saucy smile. "How do you stay so slim? You eat like a horse and the most exercise I've seen out of you is shuffling a deck of cards."

"Genetically blessed, I guess."

"Fast metabolism, gorgeous eyes and super con abilities. What a great gene pool," Danita said, wide-eyed.

"I can juggle, too."

They were still teasing and laughing when Danita pulled into a parking spot in front of the Black Oak diner.

"Okay, so you can juggle, cook the perfect omelet and do crossword puzzles in pen," she acknowledged. "I still say my playing the recorder, being able to speak horse Latin and that I can write my name with my toes beats that."

"You show me what else you can do with your toes," he

said joining her on the sidewalk and pulling her tight against him, "and I'll give you the win."

Before he could offer up a few ideas that were probably listed in the monthly foot fetish newsletter, someone stepped between them and the diner door.

"Good morning."

They both stopped short. Danita's hand dropped from his waist so fast, he was surprised his jeans didn't scrape skin off her palm. He almost shivered, both from the sudden distance between their bodies and from the chill she threw up between them. Unfamiliar with rejection by any woman, let alone one who'd sucked him dry only hours before, Gabriel stiffened. Anger sparked low in his belly, but unlike the woman looking horrified next to him, he kept his expression neutral.

"Hunter," she greeted with a shaky smile. "What a surprise."

A surprise indeed. Gabriel considered the FBI special agent. He supposed the jeans and lack of tie were supposed to be casual, but the guy still screamed uptight control.

Was he here to check up on the situation? Had he found some evidence? Something new? And more to the point, was it going to screw up Gabriel's plans or point yet another finger at his father?

Hunter's face was completely unreadable, though.

"After your call for help, I thought it was time to offer a little personal focus to this case," the other man said to Danita.

"Call for help?" Gabriel asked.

Wincing as if she realized she was stuck between an angry rock and indecipherable hard place, Danita looked at Gabriel.

"I was, am, concerned that we're not doing enough in the case. We seem to have gathered all the information available. I felt it was time to take action," she said quietly so the couple skirting around them to the diner couldn't hear.

Gabriel caught the hint of guilt in her voice, worry in her eyes. Good. She should feel both. They were supposed to be working together on this, and she'd cut him out. He'd cut her out, too, but that was beside the point. He had more on the line here.

"Clearly we all have things to talk about," Hunter said. He gestured up the block, indicating they head toward the sheriff's office. "We can use Caleb's office."

Gabriel stopped pouting over the kicks to his ego and wanted to pull Danita aside to demand just where her loyalties were. "How do you know my brother?"

Nobody but a friend would refer to Caleb by his first name. And sad to say, big brother being such a hard-ass, he had very few real friends. Gabriel's eyes narrowed as he tried to pull together the pieces of a puzzle he was realizing was much more complex than he'd realized.

So, what the hell was going on? From the look on Hunter's face, he knew and wasn't saying.

"Sorry to interrupt your breakfast plans, but I prefer privacy," Hunter murmured as they made their way down the sidewalk toward the sheriff's office with its old-fashioned wooden sign swaying in the breeze.

"No problem. I've lost my appetite," Gabriel said.

He didn't need to look at her to know she was glaring at him. He didn't care. She was the one turning that sweet expression of sexual delight between them into something to be ashamed of. Suddenly everything between them—the connection, the emotions, even the sex, clearly they'd been sidelined. Danita, or should he say Special Agent Cruz, was in full FBI mode now.

Missing her and frustrated that it hurt so much, he held open the door for Danita, then Hunter to enter the sheriff's office ahead of him. He thought it a good sign that they didn't insist he go first, like some petty thief they didn't trust.

And if he were honest, at least with himself, he'd admit a part of him did want to let the door slam shut behind them so he could take off.

Not because he was afraid of arrest.

But because now that the moment of truth had arrived, he was just a little worried whether he could afford the cost of reckoning.

"C'mon in," Caleb greeted from behind his desk. Despite how serious he knew the situation was, Gabriel still snickered at the sight of his badass brother looking all official and upright with his stack of paperwork.

Then he saw the large pink donut box on the desk next to the coffeepot and tray of mugs and rolled his eyes. "You're becoming a cliché, big brother."

"I'm not the one who was just escorted into jail by two officers of the law, little brother." Caleb's tone was light, but there was a clear warning and hint of worry in his eyes.

Gabriel's grin faded. Clearly Hunter had already visited to clue Caleb in with the down low, obviously outing Danita as an agent and as Gabriel's legal babysitter.

"I wouldn't say escorted," Gabriel corrected meticulously, hunching his shoulders at Caleb's reference to his arrest. Once Tobias was cleared of suspicion, Gabriel would be the only one left in his family on the questionable side of the law. That had never bothered him before. But now, faced with family judgment, he cringed.

He glanced at Danita, who'd refused the offer of a donut or coffee, instead sitting on one of the interview chairs, clearly letting Hunter take the lead in this little scene.

"So tell me," Gabriel said, making a show of a chocolate-covered old-fashioned donut before shooting Hunter a look over the pink lid, "how do you know Caleb? Cop school? Inter-department drug bust? Strip club buddies?"

And did Danita know? Had she kept this from him? He

hated that he couldn't read her now that she has her federal agent face on.

Caleb and Hunter, clearly anted up for the bigger game, both smiled. Caleb leaned back, the old wooden office chair squeaking as he gestured to Hunter to take the lead.

"College, actually," Hunter said. "We were roommates."

A vague recollection of a comment here and there from his brother in his rare visits home surfaced. "Your dad was FBI, too, right?"

And why had this been kept a secret? If Hunter already had an in with Caleb, why'd they use Danita as bait to get Gabriel involved? What was the bigger game?

Hunter's expression, amused till now, shuttered. With a short nod, he gestured to Caleb and changed the subject. "Caleb is assisting in this case. Like you, it's in his interest to clear your father's name. Now that he's settling in, he also has a vested concern in the town and keeping things clean here."

"Vested enough to be willing to juggle this and his upcoming nuptials at the same time, it seems," Gabriel said with an arch look at his brother. "Aren't you the clever multitasker?"

"Must be a family trait."

Gabriel's smile dimmed as those words brought back Danita's teasing that morning. Most of his life, he'd reveled in his heritage. Now he was wondering what it meant for his future. He was the last of his family to hold tight to the legacy his father had handed down. Was it time to let go?

Hell, even his father had let it go.

But before he could make any decisions, before he could even contemplate his future, he had to deal with the game he was in. Which meant busting this crime ring.

"So here's the deal," he said, taking charge of the room like this was all a part of his master plan. "Whoever brought together the goon squad wants to grab control of the major crime venues, starting here in Central California, then moving north. Each of the participants brings a specific skill to the table, and each one basically auditioned for their part by proving themselves in a series of crimes."

Brow arched, he tossed the ball to Danita. Stepping right into agent mode, she rose and faced Hunter.

"I've compiled a list of crimes I feel can safely be attributed to four of the six major players. Guns, drugs, identity theft and racketeering. The other two players are less inclined to bragging, but I suspect them of human trafficking and prostitution."

"You can tie four of them to specific unsolved crimes?" Hunter clarified.

"I can," she said with a quick nod. She pulled her cell phone out of her purse, tapped a couple of buttons, then looked back at Hunter. "I've forwarded you my notes."

"And you've had no luck breaking through to the leader?"

"No," she said with a grimace. "Not yet."

"Maybe," Gabriel answered at the same time.

With everyone's gaze on him in varying degrees of curiosity, Gabriel shifted so he wasn't directly facing Danita. She wasn't going to take this well, and as much as he believed in facing things head-on, facing a woman's fury was never easy.

"I realized that the only way to break through the barrier around the goon pack was to offer up something they needed. And couldn't get."

Danita's hiss was cut short by the loud snapping of teeth, while Hunter simply shifted his stance. Clearly the official contingent in the room weren't big on ingenuity.

"What'd you do?" Caleb finally asked, giving voice to the unspoken question hanging in the air.

"I offered a bribe."

"You offered…" Apparently overcome, and probably not with awe, Danita's words trailed off. Fists clenched, she shook her head as if she couldn't believe what she was hearing. "How could you do that? I told you, multiple times, that we were here to gather information. Not to take action. Especially not without consulting me first."

Guilt was an ugly and unfamiliar sensation, biting at Gabriel with vicious, cutting teeth. What the hell was he supposed to have done? They'd blackmailed him into this situation, he hadn't asked to come play nice with the feebies. So he'd done exactly what they should have expected. He'd played by his own rules.

He could admit, if only to himself, that he seriously regretted that those rules might hurt Danita in any way, though.

"I had a hunch and I played it. If it works out, I was going to tell you. If it doesn't, nothing was lost, right?"

Except, apparently, her trust.

Fighting the unfamiliar edge of panic that was prodding those guilty teeth into biting harder at his ass, Gabriel forced himself to focus on Caleb and Hunter instead of Danita.

"So what was your hunch, how did you play it and when will you know the results?" Hunter asked quietly. It was hard to tell if the guy was pissed or not. He played it close to the vest. But he seemed open to any opportunity, which Gabriel had to admire.

"I offered a payment of fifty grand to the cause, with another million payable in a face-to-face visit."

"A million fifty?" Caleb whistled.

"You used your own money to bribe your way into the higher echelons of this crime ring?" Hunter clarified in a biting tone that for the first time showed the guy had emotions.

Caleb winced. Gabriel could almost see his brother running legalities in his head.

"Not my money. I assume you've been monitoring my accounts since the, ahem, *arrest*." Which still grated. "No.

When I realized it was going to take something big to get the boss's attention. I used a connection of mine to access a large amount of virtually undetectable, yet very special cash."

Hunter was quick. Both brows rose and he gave a low whistle of his own. "You bribed them with counterfeit money? Traceable, counterfeit currency?"

"I handed over the first installment to Ham Bollinger last night with instructions that the other half would only be offered face-to-face. I'm pretty sure his office is bugged, something he's aware of. So the message was delivered. But even if they don't take the bait, we can still make the bust. All we have to do is wait for the initial cash to hit the streets, then trace it back to the source."

Gabriel refrained from buffing his nails on his shirt.

"And the million? Is that in counterfeit, too?"

"Nah. That part was a bluff," he said. Pulling out his wallet, he offered Hunter a hundred. "But here's a sample of the goods I handed over. I've got a few more for quality control purposes and tracking, of course."

The FBI agent inspected the bill with narrowed eyes, his brow furrowed as he tried to tell that it was fake.

"How—"

Gabriel stepped closer, silently pointing out the tells.

"Impressive," Hunter breathed. Then he gave Gabriel a hard look. "I'd like to know where you got this."

"You could ask."

Everyone in the room knew he wouldn't tell, though.

"Fine. It looks we're about to break this case wide-open then," Hunter said. Then he inclined his head toward Caleb. "Can you handle this or should I bring in backup?"

After a long, considering look, Caleb shrugged. "No problem. But just so ya know, if you screw up the wedding, Cassiopeia is likely to put a curse on all of you."

Everyone in the room grimaced.

"We won't ruin your party, Caleb," Hunter promised. Then, with the smallest wince, he added, "But if we do, I'll take responsibility with Mrs. Easton."

"Nothing's going to go wrong," Gabriel assured them. Not because he was sure. But worrying, especially about an angry mother's curse, would mess with people's performance.

And now that rehearsals were over, every performance was vital.

Steeling himself, he let his gaze move to the corner of the room where Danita sat. Arms crossed tight over her chest, knees locked together, her body language shouted "fuck you." Her glare echoed that message, blue eyes narrowed in fury whenever they landed on Gabriel.

As panic gripped his guts, tying his intestines into knots, he promised himself he'd find a way to fix it with her. Somehow.

He had to.

They had a cat counting on them. And, he grimaced, his future happiness.

FURY HAD ITS OWN flavor. Nasty, bitter and cloying. Danita almost choked on it. But no matter how many times she swallowed, she couldn't clear it away.

How dare he? She'd told him to fish for information. She'd lowered her guard and trusted him. And in return, he'd gone behind her back, using illegal means to bribe a suspect.

Clearly he had no respect for her. Not as a federal agent, and not as a woman. Otherwise, he'd have been honest.

She'd known going in that he was a player. That he was a man who could lie with the best of them and would play her and everyone around in order to get what he wanted.

Still, she had to blink hard to clear the burning tears from her eyes. Had she really believed that incredible sex was going to change the man? A leopard's spots weren't kept in his dick, spewed out with his orgasms.

"Danita, you're the agent leading this investigation. It's your bust. I suggest you check the bank. Local merchants will be making deposits and maybe we'll get lucky, find a connection."

Her throat too tight with tears to let any words pass, Danita nodded instead. Humiliation vied with the betrayal in her stomach. Hunter had trained her. He'd trusted her. And she'd blown it. She'd been so enamored with Gabriel, so busy falling in love like an idiot, that she'd overlooked one vital fact. Gabriel was in her custody, and she was only here to do a job.

Taking the lead—because it was his role or because she'd blown it?—Hunter continued to outline plans with Caleb for coordinating local efforts.

"Any input, Danita?" Hunter asked quietly.

She yanked herself back into focus. As Hunter said, she was supposed to be the FBI agent leading this investigation. And from now on, that's all she was.

"I think the counterfeit bribe does have potential to flush out the mastermind behind this, eventually. But that's not going to help us now."

"Why?" Gabriel asked, sounding offended.

Danita didn't even look at him. Instead she kept her focus on Hunter, with a glance once in a while for Caleb who was standing silent by the corner of his desk, his arms crossed as he looked her over like she were the criminal here, instead of his brother.

"You're overlooking the proposed meet for the second half of the money. If the mastermind is Tobias Black, he'll refuse the meet."

"It's not my father," Gabriel snapped.

"We don't have proof of that. As far as the FBI is concerned, he's still the primary suspect," she shot back. Her heart ached for the hurt in his eyes. The ache faded fast as his worry turned into a glare.

"The FBI? Or you?" he asked, looking as betrayed as she felt.

Danita dismissed his question with a shrug. As of now, the two were one and the same.

"But even if it's not Tobias," she continued, directing her words toward Hunter, "a refusal won't guarantee us a name. Just like the money, if found in someone's possession it could provide a break but it doesn't ensure that person is the mastermind. Only that they somehow came into the counterfeit money."

"Aren't you the soul of optimism?" Gabriel growled. Out of the corner of her eye, she saw him throw himself into a chair in front of the sheriff's desk.

"As Sheriff Black said, we are working on a deadline. This has to be resolved before the wedding, in three days. After that, there's no reason for Gabriel, or myself, to be in Black Oak."

"Then it's in our best interest to track this counterfeit money, to find a way to break Ham Bollinger and to follow all other leads to close this case," Hunter said, making it sound as easy as ordering up breakfast.

"I'm going to be busy then," she said. Her face tightened, but using all her skill, she kept the anger from showing. "It'd be best if I shift from undercover and operate behind the scenes, I think. There's no more information be gathered by pretending."

In other words, she wanted to be in a separate room, a separate hotel and preferably a separate state from Gabriel Black.

"You need to stay undercover until we close the case," Hunter said quietly. Danita sucked in a breath, ready to argue, but the look he gave her made her settle back in her chair. He was right. Giving away her role here would only tip off the crime boss. But she'd be damned if she was spending any more time with Gabriel than necessary. "Update your reports, put a trace on the counterfeit money and confer with Gabriel to solidify our next steps. I'll expect a briefing from you in three hours."

"What'll you be doing?" she asked, knowing the question was out of line but not wanting to be alone with Gabriel yet. Not until she had a handle on her temper and could override the feeling of betrayal that had misery coursing through her.

Hunter flashed a quick smile filled with charm and amusement. "I've got to get fitted for my tux. Wedding's in three days and I'm one of the groomsmen."

Damn. There went her buffer.

Steeling herself, she looked toward Gabriel. He clearly still had an issue with her outburst if the cold look he speared her with was any indication.

Goody. Nothing said a strong working relationship like iced-over fury.

"I'll show you to the tailors," Gabriel told Hunter. He gave Danita an undecipherable look then added, "I think Danita might want some privacy to do all that busywork."

Her hiss was obscured by the rush of male feet, all scurrying toward the door like rats deserting an angry woman about to set their damned ship on fire.

On his way past, Caleb handed her a slip of paper.

"Computer access passwords," he said, the charm in his smile rivaling his rat fink of a brother's. "I figure you can get that privacy in here without a problem.

And just like that, they were gone.

Her boss, her liaison and her lover.

Leaving Danita the privacy Gabriel had mentioned, and the freedom to finally let the tears fall.

She'd always known she was skating a thin line between

her career and her relationship with Gabriel. And she'd assured herself, over and over, that her career would always come first.

Too bad she hadn't realize how much it'd hurt to have to choose between that career and the man she loved.

12

WORK. THAT'S ALL she could count on, and from now on, all she should care about. Danita ground her teeth to keep the tears at bay as she silently chanted that reminder. Gabriel had distracted her with sex and cats and the lure of a family. And all the while, he'd been conning her.

Using her.

Determined to prove she wasn't as incompetent as he must think her, she followed Hunter's orders and used Caleb's secure computer to type her notes up into an official report. An hour later, as her fingers flew over the keyboard, she was viciously aware of Caleb's presence.

Why had he returned? Shouldn't he be supervising tuxedo fittings or filling Hunter in on groomsman duties? Groomsman, she thought with a surge of confused anger. Why hadn't Hunter let her know he had a personal connection on this case? Because he didn't trust her? Had he expected—rightfully—for her to screw up?

She wanted to beat on the keyboard, but figured abusing city property might irk the good sheriff.

Finally she couldn't stand it. She glanced over and met Caleb's eyes. They were so like Gabriel's. Her heart stuttered a little at the look he was giving her. Long, intense and unblinking.

Those Black boys definitely had a lot in common.

"You have something you'd like to say?" she prodded.

"Just wondering how you're holding up."

"How *I'm* holding up?" she asked, leaning away from the computer to frown at him. "Why?"

"So suspicious?" He took his time pouring two cups of coffee then brought them over, setting one on the desk in front of her. "Why wouldn't I be curious about your state of mind? You're clearly a vital force in this case. Both my father's innocence and my brother's safety depend on your discernment and clear thinking, don't they?"

Her spine rigid, she shifted her shoulders and lifted her chin. She felt like she was giving testimony before an aggressively ambitious prosecutor. A part of her, the part that still saw Caleb as her lover's brother, wanted to tell him to back off. But the rest of her, the part that valued her career, realized that this was a coordinated investigation with a great deal on the line.

"You don't have to worry about me doing my job," she assured Caleb. Not liking the disadvantage of sitting there like she was in detention, Danita pushed away from the desk. With a nod of thanks, she took the coffee to the side table and added cream. Then, both to make a show of nonchalance and because it was chocolate, dammit, she selected a chocolate-glazed old-fashioned out of the donut box.

"How long have you known the FBI had an investigation open on your father?" she asked, taking the offensive along with a seat on the edge of the desk. "Clearly you and Hunter have a history. He's even in your wedding, which appears to be quite the surprise for your best man. Does that history extend to forgiving an intrusion of this level?"

"There's nothing to forgive," Caleb said with a shrug. "I

believe in the role of law enforcement. And I spent enough years undercover to know that a lot more gets done covertly than through official channels."

Danita gave him her sweetest smile before nibbling an edge off her donut. "You didn't answer my question, though. Did you know about the investigation? Were you clued in that I was FBI when we arrived?"

Caleb's own smile was more wicked than sweet. The look he gave her was long and searching, as if he were trying to see, not into her work ethics, but into her heart.

"Let's just say that as the person in charge of enforcing law in Black Oak, I prefer to know as much about what's going on here as possible."

He'd known.

Her heart ached for Gabriel. How would he feel when he found out his brother had been playing him? He had no room to complain, given that he had played his entire family with their false engagement. But she knew he'd be hurt.

"Apparently your family is quite gifted at lying to each other. And to others," she added before she could stop herself.

"I guess we are. But only when it's justified." Caleb took his time refreshing his coffee. "You know, I essentially lied to Pandora when I came to town. I can justify it with the excuse that I was on a case. But the results are the same."

"I didn't lie to Gabriel."

"No, but you did to everyone else under the guise of it just being your job, right?"

She opened her mouth to protest that she hadn't slept with everyone else, hadn't given her heart to any of them. Then she snapped it shut. Did it matter? Lying was lying.

"I'm sure, in the end, if you ask Gabriel, he'll tell you that all of this—" he gestured to the room where they'd had their little powwow two hours before "—was just him doing his job."

"It's not the same."

"No? Let's set aside the physical risk factor for a second, since in this case Gabriel's life was right there on the line next to yours."

He waited, for what she wasn't sure. Finally, frustrated, Danita gave a nod. Apparently that's all he'd wanted, because Caleb nodded back, then continued, "Because when you do your job, you have, what…your reputation on the line?"

"I'd like to think I've devoted my life to my career for more than building a reputation," she snapped. "This isn't about my ego."

"I'm sure it's not," he said agreeably. "But let's be honest. In this situation, Gabriel had a lot more at risk than reputation. Or whatever time he'd have served if he didn't scream entrapment instead of going along with Hunter's plan."

She sniffed, knowing that line of entrapment versus arrest was very blurry in Gabriel's case. Still, he'd gone along. With a little extra incentive, of course. She dropped her gaze from Caleb's to the vivid pink of her pointy-toed pumps. She had a feeling that extra incentive was going to be Caleb's point.

"Failure to solve this case will be a smudge on your record. Failure for Gabriel means our father will be locked up for the rest of his life." He paused for a sip of coffee. Danita thought it was for effect at first, then she saw the tension in his fingers clenched on the mug. He was just as worried as Gabriel. Maya must be as well. Danita's heart clenched. As contentious as it might look from the outside, this was a family that all loved each other very much.

"So you might be mad that he took a few extra steps, hedged his bets, so to speak. But consider his reasons."

She understood them. She could even accept them.

But she also had to accept the fact that they were proof-positive that she and Gabriel had no future. That he operated on the opposite side of the law.

It wasn't her pride that was aching, she realized. It was her heart.

"When we initiated this investigation I didn't realize he cared about his family," she said quietly. "Not at first. He cut ties, walked away. Our reports show you've all been estranged for almost a decade."

"We're a stubborn bunch," Caleb agreed. "But that doesn't mean we don't care, a hell of a lot, about each other. Just because Gabriel was trying to prove something, that doesn't mean he doesn't love our father."

She nodded. "I realized that. After we got here. After I saw all of you together."

"Then you shouldn't hold his actions against him."

"You wouldn't be trying to convince me that Gabriel would have been all up-front and honest, laying all his cards on the table, if his father wasn't the suspect?"

Caleb's smile was wider than his brother's. Edgier, with a hint of wicked where Gabriel's was pure charm. But the way it lit his eyes was exactly the same when he laughed.

"Oh no. Like you said, lying is an art form in our family. It's a part of the job." The look he gave her was pointed and painful. "You should know that. I'd say you are pretty skilled in that department yourself."

"I didn't lie to Gabriel," she snapped before she could stop herself. "He knew, from the beginning, what my job was. What I was here to do. He was aware that we suspect your father, and he was clear on the parameters of this case."

"And you were clear on his." Caleb gave her a long look, then with a deep breath said, "We don't know who's behind this. My father pulled strings to get Hunter, and in turn you, involved in this case. He says he did it to clear his name. He's good enough that that, too, could be a con. But I have to believe it isn't. And I know Gabriel, even though he knows we lied to him, will have to believe that, too."

Caleb surprised her with a friendly pat on the shoulder before he turned to leave.

Danita dropped into the chair she'd vacated earlier. She didn't know how long she stared at the blurred computer screen after the sound of the closing door signaled Caleb's departure. His words, spoken and unspoken, rang through her mind.

She had a choice. She could give in to the aching demand of her heart. Or she could be true to herself and follow her career.

But could she live the rest of her life loving someone who operated on the wrong side of the law? Someone who epitomized everything she'd sworn to fight? Even if he gave it all up, could she trust him? What did they really have between them? Hot sex and a quirky cat?

She loved Gabriel. There was no question of that. But how long could she live with him if she gave up her job, her beliefs and her future?

And how long could she live with herself if she didn't?

Tears tracked, unchecked down her cheeks as she struggled to accept the truth.

She couldn't spend her life with him.

But she could make his life a little easier. She'd clear his father, give him his family back. And then she'd say goodbye.

Blinking away useless tears, she sucked in a shaky breath and got to work. She finished typing up her last report and added it to the FBI case file. Now she needed to check on the money.

She called Hunter.

"What protocol would you prefer I follow with the bank? Do you want me to maintain cover?"

"We don't have time. I'll run the bank owner for security clearance. Wait for my go-ahead."

In typical Hunter fashion, she had the go-ahead text within ten minutes. She left the sheriff's department to take the short stroll toward the bank. It was doubtful anyone would be stupid enough to make that large a cash deposit. But still, she'd cover all the bases.

"I'm Agent Cruz," she said twenty minutes later, introducing herself once she'd reached the privacy of the bank president's office. She went on to explain the situation—stressing the need for confidentiality—before requesting access to the bank's cash vault. Like any good banker, Waxman, the president, first called the sheriff for verification, then the local FBI office as well. A half hour later, he gave her access to a small ATM vault and that morning's deposits.

"Why don't we start back here? It's quieter and less obtrusive," Mr. Waxman said, gesturing to a small room. "We haven't sorted our night deposits yet. Please, don't take offense, but I'll stay with you as you make your inspection."

"Of course," Danita agreed with a cool smile as she took a seat and pulled the first deposit bag toward her. Thirty minutes later, she'd learned to block out the sound of Waxman's fingers tapping "Twinkle Twinkle Little Star" on the table.

Not even seeing the denominations any longer, her eyes blurred as she flipped through the serial numbers. This was such a waste of time.

Then something caught her eye. She pulled a twenty out of the rubber-banded stack of bills. Eyes narrowed, she inspected it. Pre-1998 currency redesign, the bill was soft with age. The color was perfect, as was the artwork. But there, just on the edge of the four in the serial number, was a pale line. As if the printing plate was missing ink.

Excitement zinged.

"Mr. Waxman, can you tell me which account this is?" she

asked, indicating a large vinyl envelope. "The slip indicates an account number, but no name."

He glanced at the slip, and obviously a credit to the small town, didn't even have to look up the account number.

"That's the Forever in Joy account. Our local wedding planner, Lisa Duffy."

Wedding planner? Danita's stomach pitched. Biting her lip, she held the bill up to the light, confirming the slight tell Gabriel had warned them of.

And she remembered Maya explaining why Cassiopeia had gone overboard with pre-wedding parties.

Because Tobias was covering all of the wedding costs.

NOW AT YET ANOTHER freaking wedding party, this time the rehearsal celebration at his father's, Gabriel was going crazy. He'd known she'd be pissed over his sidestepping her in the case, but he hadn't thought she'd close him out completely.

It'd been a day and a half since he'd seen Danita, except at a distance. When he'd returned to the manor her bags, and the cat, were gone. He'd heard later that she'd checked into the inn using the public excuse that they'd had a tiff. Caleb said she'd agreed to close the case and stay undercover, but had told Hunter that she needed distance.

Distance, hell. She was plotting to arrest his father and didn't want him watching. Or, he sighed, Hunter's arrival had reminded her that she was a Fed and Gabriel was criminally off-limits.

"Anger like that's gonna eat your insides up."

So focused on his tiny world of misery, Gabriel hadn't heard his father come up behind him. It was a sad state of affairs that pouting over Danita had put him in a heartbroken fog.

"I'm not angry," he denied, trying not to wince at the possibility of being struck down by lightning for lying right to his father's face.

Tobias arched one brow and waited.

Gabriel shrugged, then blurted out, "More stressed than angry, I guess. I'm committed to a game that's out of control and I'm on the wrong side of the odds."

"Son, let me give you some advice."

Despite the heaviness weighing on him, Gabriel grinned. When he'd wanted to play guitar, he'd been advised to consider the necessary hours of practice required to play "Stairway to Heaven." When he'd been considering how he'd get sweet Anna McGee to offer him his first taste of heaven, he'd been advised to worry more about her hearing angels than himself. And when he'd told his old man he was through with him, that he was leaving home and wouldn't return until he'd proved himself the better man, he'd been advised to be careful what he wished for. Because all wishes came with a price.

"Go ahead, Dad. Give me some advice," he invited.

"Sometimes the hand we're dealt is a challenge. It pushes us to level up, to risk more. Sometimes a questionable hand is a warning. It gives us a chance to rethink the game and our direction. And sometimes," he added with a look that saw straight to Gabriel's heart, and quite possibly through to his soul, "sometimes it's just time to find a new game."

Gabriel set his beer aside and shoved both hands into the front pockets of his slacks. His heartbeat sped as he worked to keep his expression calm. This was it. He'd have plenty of times in the future to change his mind, but he knew, in his heart, that this was the crossroads.

"I guess it's time to get out of the game," he finally said. Unfamiliar shame and a sort of melancholy rolled over him. He'd failed. He'd left home vowing to be a bigger con, a better criminal than his father. He'd never held a real job, had no actual training. And he was quitting? Was he insane?

He met his father's discerning gaze with resignation. Failure wasn't a good feeling.

"I'm proud of you, Gabriel," Tobias said quietly. So quietly, Gabriel cocked his head and wondered if his ears were playing tricks.

"Beg pardon?"

"That's a hard decision to make. Given your talents and brain, you're walking away from something with a huge potential. And you're doing it for the right reasons. That's a hard thing to do. You make me proud."

"Well." Stumped, Gabriel had nothing to say. It wasn't every day an overachieving father congratulated his son for being a quitter.

Before he could fumble his way through the emotions clogging his throat, there was a commotion at the entry to the living room. He was grateful. Right up until he saw who was causing the ruckus.

Shit. He'd been waiting and hoping. But now he wasn't ready to see her.

"Some women take your breath away," Tobias said, observing Danita's entrance on Hunter's arm. "You got yourself a nice one there, son. Worth giving up the game for."

Gabriel winced. Caleb was in the know because of his job as town law. But in typical close-to-the-vest Black fashion, he'd clearly kept that knowledge to himself. And Gabriel had been too busy licking his wounds to admit to the family that his true love was a total fake. That Danita was only playing the loving fiancée in hopes of slapping the cuffs on his father.

"I'm not doing it for her," he said with a grimace. Because he knew damned well he would have. But she wouldn't have him, either way. And he couldn't have a woman whose life ambition was to ruin his family.

Even if he wanted her more than he wanted his next breath.

"Interesting, her showing up with Caleb's old college buddy," Tobias contemplated.

Shit.

"They know each other," was all Gabriel could say.

Shoulder to shoulder, he and his father watched Danita and Hunter approach the happy groom-to-be. Gabriel frowned at the intensity on her face. Closed, professional with just a hint of chill.

Something had broke.

All he needed to see was Caleb's wince to know that it was something big. Three pair of eyes cut to Tobias, but Gabriel kept his attention on his brother. There was pain in his face. Tension in his shoulders. And a sadness that made Gabriel's stomach pitch.

This wasn't going to be good.

His stomach, already in his throat, tumbled toward his belly as Caleb and Hunter made their way across the room. Danita waited at the entrance. Whether she was standing guard or preparing to run was anyone's guess.

"Hello," Tobias greeted Hunter with a handshake and a big smile. "Glad to have you here to support Caleb's big day."

"Dad, the case is breaking," Caleb murmured.

Gabriel frowned. What was going on? Had his brother actually filled their father in on the case?

"We'd like to use your study, Mr. Black," Hunter said, his tone as formal as his stance. "If you'd come with us, we can keep this from disrupting the party. And—" he cast a quick glance and wince toward Cassiopeia, who was holding court in the corner "—we can avoid upsetting the bride-to-be or her mother."

Gabriel and Caleb shared a smirk, both remembering the warning that Cassiopeia would curse whoever messed up the wedding.

Tobias's eyes circled the group, the look in them sharp. He gave a short nod, then waved his hand toward the hallway.

"Go ahead. I'll be right along."

"I'd rather you came with us now," Hunter insisted, a hint of apology in his tone.

"I'll be right along. I need to get Maya." Without waiting for a response, he turned away and melted into the crowd.

Hunter looked like he was going to follow, but Caleb shook his head.

"No. Maya should be here. She needs to hear this, too."

When Hunter didn't object, the sinking feeling in Gabriel's stomach turned to lead.

Needing a few seconds, he didn't wait for the rest of them. Instead, fists in the pockets of his slacks, Gabriel took the familiar path down the hallway toward his father's study. He felt Danita's gaze on him from across the room, but didn't look her way. And she just messed up his head in all sorts of ways.

He stepped into the study. It'd barely changed. The walls were lighter. The couch new. But the pictures on the wall were the same, an ode to his childhood. There, on the Chippendale executive desk, was a clumsy ceramic ashtray Maya had made in Girl Scouts, Caleb's T-ball trophy. And, Gabriel noted with a long sigh, the World's Best Dad mug he'd given Tobias one Father's Day.

How lonely was it, sitting in here with the memories of his family and nobody to share them with?

Gabriel told himself not to feel guilty. He'd had a solid reason for leaving. Just as Caleb and Maya had. It was a waste of time and energy to regret choices made long ago. But the one he'd made a week ago? To bring Danita and the FBI into his father's house? That choice was eating at his guts.

Before he could sink too far into the stress of it, she

stepped into the room. His family and Hunter quickly followed, with Hunter shutting the door behind him.

In typical fashion, Tobias took his seat behind the desk. The center of command, in the room, in the house and in the lives of his family.

"Danita," Hunter said once everyone had settled. "Please report."

Gabriel sighed. At least whatever horrible news she was about to share would overshadow the fact that Danita was about to blow the cover on their fake engagement.

Grief surged as he watched her sever that last, fake tie between them.

"I was instructed to discover the mastermind behind the crimes being perpetrated here in Black Oak," Danita said to the room at large. She continued in that same distant tone, laying the groundwork of what her job was and the FBI's purpose for sending her. Gabriel ignored the looks his family sent his way, instead focusing completely on Danita. What did she know? And why the hell was she taking so long to tell them?

"The counterfeit currency Gabriel used to set up the criminal boss surfaced at the bank yesterday," Danita continued in a neutral tone. "We followed the deposit."

The room felt like it was charged with electricity as everyone waited while Danita paused to take a deep breath. She clenched both hands together before unlacing her fingers and lifting her hands in a half-shrug. "The money was deposited by Forever in Joy. It was used in payment for the Easton-Black wedding."

In a shot, Maya was on her feet, her protests loud and passionate. Caleb grabbed her arm with a warning not to make them regret bringing her in. Hunter leaned against the door, watching.

Tobias simply steepled his fingers, elbows propped on his desk as he watched the show with interest.

"That's crap." Gabriel's quiet words did more to calm her sister than any of Caleb's threats. "You're trying to pin my brother now? Or, what? Cassiopeia?"

"No." Hands now grasped behind her back, Danita paced in front of Tobias's desk as she finished reporting. "Pandora told me that Tobias is paying for the wedding as his gift. So all of the funds should be traceable directly to him."

"That's bullshit," Gabriel said, anger clear in his tone.

"Actually," Danita said quietly, slowly as if she were tip-toeing her way through the words to make sure she didn't step in the wrong one, "there's more."

"More?" Maya hissed, sounding like a furious cat ready to pounce with claws bared. "How much more damage do you need to do? You were supposed to come here and clear my father. Now you're trying to arrest him?"

"Wait," Gabriel said, raising his palm toward Danita to stop her defense. "What do you mean, she was supposed to clear Dad's name? What do you know about this, Maya?"

His sister winced, then lifted her chin and pressed her lips together. Fury was an edgy layer over the worry and frustration already roiling in his belly.

He didn't bother looking toward his father. He'd get nothing there. Instead his gaze shot to Caleb. Almost as inscrutable as Tobias. Still, there was a hint of something in Caleb's eyes.

"This was a setup?" Gabriel's glare shot between his brother and Hunter. "All of you? You were all in on it? What the hell was the point? Do you all just lie for the fun of it now?"

"Don't jump to conclusions," Caleb warned.

"Did you know that Hunter was involved in a case against Dad before I came home?" Gabriel asked directly. Caleb was hell on wheels with prevarication. But a direct lie? Harder between brothers. "Did you know Danita was FBI when we came to town?"

"Hey," Maya interceded, jumping to the defense of the underdog as usual. "You're the one who claimed her for your fiancée. What's with that lie? You're not lily-white, Gabriel, so watch how you point those fingers."

In two seconds, he and his sister were yelling in each other's faces with Caleb alternating between accuser and peacemaker. Tobias, as he always had in his children's arguments, simply leaned back in his chair and waited.

The feebies weren't as patient, apparently. Within minutes, Hunter grasped Gabriel's arm and Danita pulled Maya's finger out of his chest.

"I'm sorry," Hunter interrupted. "I know this is an important family issue. And one that clearly needs to be addressed. But at this moment, our FBI case does need to take precedence. I'd like Agent Cruz to complete her report."

Gabriel didn't give a good damn what Hunter wanted. He almost said that, too, but Caleb's glare made him snap his mouth shut. Fine. He'd wait until they dealt with this little problem. Then he'd show his brother and sister just how good he'd gotten at ass-kicking in the last few years.

"Say what you want, but the reports are bullshit," Gabriel said, finally finding his voice in the face of the barrage of betrayals. "I don't care who got their hands on the counterfeit cash. It's not our father."

Danita finally met his gaze, misery clear in the blue depths of her eyes. There was an understanding on her face, and an apology.

An hour ago, he'd have given anything to see the understanding. Now? He didn't want it or that damned apology.

"It's a well-crafted setup," she agreed, surprising him. And

Maya, if his little sister's gasp was any indication. "But it is, clearly, a setup."

"You know it's not my father?" Relief was a tidal wave, almost kicking Gabriel off his feet.

"Everything your father has paid for, to date, is by check. There's no reason to believe that he'd suddenly change his MO and pay with cash."

"That's not proof."

Gabriel glared at Caleb. Was he trying to ruin their father's vindication?

"No. That isn't proof. But I talked to Lisa Duffy, the business owner, to check into the payment."

"And?"

"Gabriel," she said, something in her tone compelling, forcing him to look at her. "I'm sorry."

"Why? You cleared my father? What's there to apologize for?"

With a grimace, she glanced at Hunter. He gave her an implacable nod. Danita wet her lips, her gaze traveling from brother to sister to brother before her gaze returned to Gabriel.

"I'm sorry. But the person behind the criminal activity, the one trying to set your father up to take the fall for the drugs, the guns and even the crime ring…"

She grimaced, then as if she couldn't help herself, she reached out to take his hand.

"Gabriel, it's not your father. He's clear." She swallowed hard, then like she would rip a bandage from a wound, said it as quickly as possible. "The person behind the crimes is your aunt."

13

STARING OUT OVER his father's backyard, Gabriel let the night air comfort him. Was this what karma felt like? After years of conning people without compunction, he found himself having been conned on so many levels, he couldn't separate them all.

Here he'd thought if he got out of the game now, he'd be getting out a winner.

But one way or another, fate always demanded payment.

He heard the soft click of heels against the slate of the patio but didn't turn. Maybe if he ignored them, whoever it was would take a hint and go away.

"Gabriel?"

And there it was. All that anger he'd been wishing for. He'd just needed Danita to ignite it.

"I'd rather be alone right now," he said quietly, hoping she'd take the hint before the anger got a serious hold.

"Are you okay?"

Gabriel pulled his gaze away from the tree house flanking the tall oak in his father's backyard and glanced through the dark at her. The chilly February night hadn't been conducive to an outdoor party, so there were not pretty lights or music out here like there was inside.

"Your father asked me to find you," she said when he remained silent. "Things are coming to a head and he felt you'd want to be brought up to date."

"Funny how people suddenly think I should be in the know now. Where was their concern last week? Last month?"

"You have a right to your anger," she said slowly, in that careful tone she'd probably been trained to use when dealing with deranged criminals. "But you might want to keep in mind that as reticent as your family was, you were equally unforthcoming in your own dealings with others."

"You mean my dealings with you," he corrected. "You're pissed about the counterfeit deal. Even though it broke the case."

Accepting that she wouldn't go away, and realizing he had a few things to say now that he had her attention, he turned to face her. Always the tough gal, Danita stared right back. He could see her own anger in her eyes, but it was buried there under all that professionalism she liked to hide behind.

Suddenly he wanted nothing more than to bust that professionalism all to hell and see the real her. To find out if he'd ever known the real her. Or was she always playing a role, even when they'd made love?

"You should have told me," she pointed out in that cool, condescending tone he remembered from their meeting in Hunter's office weeks ago. "You could have jeopardized everything, including your father's safety."

"Wasn't your main goal in coming here to arrest my father? You don't care if I jeopardized his safety. You're just pissed that I jeopardized your glory."

"Glory?" she breathed, her tone so hot he was surprised it wasn't accompanied by fire. "Just because you live for attention doesn't mean the rest of us do."

"And yet, here you are, all uptight and angry because you were shown up to your boss."

Her big blue eyes rounded and a hiss escaped her. He wondered if steam was next. "I am no such thing."

"You didn't come back to the manor. You stole Pippi. And worst of all, you quit sleeping with me," he accused. As soon as the words were out, he wanted them back. He didn't do this. Didn't lose control over women. Yet here he was, whining that he'd had to sleep alone last night.

Gabriel shoved his hand through his hair, barely keeping from growling. It was just as well the case was coming to a close and Danita would be leaving. She was clearly bad for his control.

"I didn't come out here to argue with you," she snapped. Then, sucking in a deep breath through her nose as if control were floating in the air around her, she pressed her lips together.

"So why'd you come out again? Why'd you sign on to any of this?" he prodded. Then he snapped his fingers, almost right under her nose. "Oh yeah. I remember now. It was your job."

"Are we going to do this?" she asked, losing her fight with control over that anger and stepping forward so they were chest-to-chest. Close enough that when she stabbed her finger into his shoulder he knew it'd leave a bruise. "You want to compare jobs? Career choices?"

"Which one of us is a better liar?" he added.

"When did I lie to you?" she demanded. He gave her an arch look, his gaze traveling from the top of the smooth waves of her hair to the tip of her sedate black pumps. "Oh, fine. I lied in the first fifteen minutes of our relationship when I, in doing my job, pretended to be a hooker. But you lied to me outside the job by not telling me about the counterfeit money."

Falling back on arrogance, he arched one brow and gave her a sneer. "That was *my* job."

"Fine. Whatever. We're one for one, each of us lying to the other."

"One, hell," he dismissed. He realized it wasn't anger pushing him now. It was hurt. "You conspired with Hunter and my father, my entire damned family, to con me. This deal wasn't cooked up in an FBI office. This entire plan is too big for that."

She lifted her chin, looking like she was going to spew a scathing protest. Then she sighed.

"You're right. At least about the bigger scope. I never understood how Hunter knew the depth of information he had to be so sure your father was innocent. I didn't agree with the parameters he put on the case, but I followed orders. I didn't realize until we were in the sheriff's office yesterday that he was tied into this with your family."

"You didn't realize it until yesterday? You say that as if you weren't a part of the bigger game. Like you're innocent somehow."

He hated how much he wanted to believe all of that.

"You don't believe me?" she asked, her voice so quiet, so drenched with hurt that Gabriel felt like a slug. Could she be that good an actress? Or was she really hurt?

A part of him wanted to hold on to the anger, to the blame. As long as he could point a finger at her, he could accept that they had no future. He could deal with the idea that she'd never welcome him into her life for the long term. For real.

Before he could grapple with the ramifications of his fears, she shook her head.

"It doesn't matter," she dismissed.

"Doesn't matter?" he sneered.

"No. Because the job is over. We're through. I'll drop Pippi off with Caleb before I leave town. I can't take on the responsibility of a pet anyway," she said, her words choked and her eyes miserable. She waved a hand between the two of them.

"This is done. So who did what, it doesn't matter. What matters is tonight."

"What's tonight?" he asked, the words bitter on his tongue.

"Hunter and Caleb conferred. They decided to make the move tonight." She hesitated. As if she really did care, her eyes turned soft as she inspected his face and gave a sympathetic grimace. "Now, actually. The majority of the guests have gone home. Maya's been keeping your aunt occupied to ensure she doesn't leave."

Gabriel's gaze cut to the house. His anger shifted, twisted. And then dissipated in a puff of realization. He was pissed at Danita, yes. Hurt, definitely. But the churning fury in his gut? That was all for his aunt.

How could she?

Images from childhood, family holiday dinners and school events, all rushed through his mind. Sure, his dad and Cynthia tended to snip and snap at each other, but he'd always figured it was normal family tension.

But a setup like this? To frame his father for extensive crimes while pulling criminal strings to the degree Cynthia had? That required hate.

And that made Gabriel unbearably sad.

As if sensing his turmoil, Danita grimaced. Her eyes softened as her entire demeanor turned sympathetic.

"Do you want to be in on the arrest?" she asked quietly, stepping close enough that the warm wildflower scent of her perfume wrapped around him.

What he wanted was one last night, twelve hours to bury himself in her body. To say goodbye to the delights they'd explored together. But it didn't look like his wants were on the agenda any longer.

So he'd settle for closure.

"Fine," he said, gesturing toward the house. "Let's get this over with."

DANITA HAD ALWAYS loved her job. It was a means of satisfaction, a place to hide and a validation of self for her. In the six years she'd been with the bureau there had, of course, been tasks she'd been less than thrilled with.

But at this moment, her job felt like a combination of cleaning a frat house, evicting the elderly and modeling leather underwear at a class reunion. In other words, disgusting, miserable and humiliating.

She stepped into the Blacks' comfortable living room just ahead of Gabriel, her eyes drawn again to the family portrait over the fireplace. It was a picnic scene. Maya looked about a year old in it as she cuddled on her mother's lap and Gabriel was a preschooler, mischief glowing from his angelic face as he stood next to his older brother, one hand on his mother's shoulder and the other gripped in his father's. Tobias, ever the patriarch, knelt behind his family with a big smile, his pleasure and joy clear.

Danita knew the death of Celia, Tobias's wife, had painfully fractured the family. Now she got to be the one to put another crack in that fragile unit.

Maybe being judged as a second-generation promiscuous loser modeling leather underwear wasn't such a bad job after all.

"Danita." Hunter's word was a greeting, a question and a command, all rolled together.

A quick glance around assured her that the room had been cleared. Cassiopeia and Pandora had gone with Simon, Maya's fiancé, the women unaware that he was providing protection just in case. Tobias sat in his easy chair, apparently at ease except for the tapping of his fingers on the worn leather.

It was time.

She took a fortifying breath, then without thought, met

Gabriel's eyes. She saw the pain and anger there. But beneath that, the acceptance.

Feeling a little less ill than she had a few seconds ago, she moved to the center of the room. Hunter shifted to block the exit, while Caleb took up position by the back door. Not that any of them really thought an almost-sixty-year-old woman was going to make a break for it. But training was training.

"Excuse me," Danita said. Her words were quiet, but their effect was explosive.

Maya gave a tiny jump. She covered it well with a cough, then an easy smile. But her nerves were evident in the way she twisted her fingers together.

Tobias simply sighed. Gabriel lifted his chin as if ready to take a blow.

The only person at ease was Cynthia Parker.

"Ms. Parker? I'd like a word, if you don't mind."

"I prefer being addressed as Your Honor, but no matter. You're practically family now, dear." The mayor's forgiveness came complete with a curious arch of her brows and polite smile. Then she looked around the room, noting the serious attitudes and tense faces. "What is it? Are you and Gabriel having a problem?"

"Actually," Danita said, "this isn't about Gabriel and me. This is regarding the criminal activities here in Black Oak."

"Indeed?" The older woman's lashes fluttered briefly before she pulled that careful smile back into place and glanced at Caleb. "I would have assumed that the law is being upheld just fine by my own nephew. If you're considering settling into Black Oak, you'll be quite safe and well taken care of here."

Danita had to hand it to her, the woman was queen of the doublespeak.

"I have every confidence in Caleb's talent to keep the law in town. You should be informed that with his cooperation, we've taken steps to ensure the continued safety and care of everyone in Black Oak."

The mayor's eyes darted around the room, a frown forming between her brows. "Who are you, exactly? What have you done?"

"Ms. Parker, I'm with the FBI."

The woman's face stiffened, but she didn't drop her smile. She really was made for politics.

"We've just arrested nine men who were staying at the Black Oak Manor, Your Honor. The primary charges include possession with intent to distribute drugs, illegal weapons and conspiracy."

"That's quite a list," Cynthia said, her eyes wide with feigned concern. Danita could see her pulse racing in her throat, though. The woman was scared.

"You might be interested in knowing we also arrested your lover, Hamilton Bollinger."

"My what?" she gasped with nicely feigned outrage. "I cannot believe you'd have the nerve to make such an accusation."

"Upon his arrest, Mr. Bollinger confessed to the relationship between the two of you."

Fury, then fear flashed across the mayor's stately face. Her eyes darted around the room, fingers trembling just a little as she pushed back her hair. Then she seemed to pull it all together, giving Danita a regal tilt of her head in acknowledgment.

"I do prefer to keep my private life private. But if we must label it, I prefer the term gentleman friend," Cynthia corrected with a chilly sniff of disdain.

"I'll make sure the defense attorneys are apprised of your preference," Danita assured her. She thought she saw Tobias's lips twitch. His children, however, all simply looked devastated. Danita's heart ached.

"You're implying that I'll need a defense?"

"Ms. Parker, you've been implicated in a number of crimes. Would you like me to list them or would you prefer to engage counsel first?"

"You dare…" It was like someone had flipped a switch. The curtain of civility flew off for just a second as the mayor jumped to her feet and sucked in a hissing breath through her teeth. Glaring at Danita, she slapped both fists on her ample hips. "Are you arresting me, young lady?"

"Yes, ma'am," Danita said with a slow nod. The apology on her face wasn't for the mayor, though. It was for the roomful of people she'd hurt by doing her job. A job she'd thought was everything to her. Until now.

"This is ridiculous," Cynthia snapped, starting to pace the room. Her hands jerked as she gestured wildly. "Do you have any idea who I am? The power I command? Perhaps you have evidence, trumped-up, no doubt, against Ham and his cohorts. But I've yet to hear where I factor into this little conspiracy theory of yours."

"If you'll take a seat, ma'am," Danita said quietly. As much to keep Cynthia from accidently—or not so accidentally—smacking someone with one of those flying hands as to bring some semblance of control back to the discussion.

"Fine," the mayor snapped, perching on the edge of her chair. "Now explain yourself."

"In an effort to both convince the kingpin that he was serious about ousting his father and stepping into a command position with this new conglomerate, Gabriel acquired a large amount of cash."

"You're telling me that my nephew is involved in these criminal activities? Is he behind it all?"

Danita almost lost it when Cynthia gave a sad shake of her head as if to say she wasn't surprised. Would this woman throw her entire family under the bus?

"No, ma'am." Danita gave Gabriel a quick look. At his infinitesimal inclination of his head, she informed his aunt, "The cash that he offered as a bribe was counterfeit. Completely traceable."

"Count…" Now the mayor looked scared. She shot a vicious glare at her nephew, then pressed both hands to her forehead for a brief second. With all the police presence in town, Cynthia must have forgotten that the money was counterfeit.

"Ma'am," Danita continued, wanting to get this over for everyone. "We obtained a search warrant for your home and office. We found the same counterfeit currency, as well as the receipt showing that you paid to have napkins with your slogan printed for Caleb's wedding, along with five large flower arrangements in your campaign colors."

The mayor licked her lips, looking around as if an explanation was painted on one of the walls.

"We also checked your campaign account. This morning, you transferred forty thousand dollars into the account as a personal contribution."

"You're mistaken," Cynthia said, her words a hoarse whisper.

"No, ma'am. I'm not. I'm sorry, but we're going to take you into custody now."

Unable to hurt these people she'd come to care about any further, Danita tossed aside pride and cast Hunter a begging look. He stepped forward to take the mayor's arm.

"If you'll come with me, ma'am," he murmured, turning her toward the exit.

"Get your hands off me," Cynthia snapped, wrenching free with a hiss of anger. "How dare you? How dare all of you? You're obstructionists is what you are. Trying to end my political career. This isn't going to work. You'll see. I will bury you."

Danita watched in growing concern as the older woman's words rose and fell, fury fueling hysteria. Accusations flew, words like *jealousy, paranoia* and *collusion* tangling in a big ugly knot of emotional blackmail.

"Why?" Maya asked, her tear-filled words stopping the angry rant. "Aunt Cynthia, why did you do it? Why would you associate with criminals? Bring them here, to Black Oak? And why would you use all of that to frame Dad?"

As though she'd just hit a wall of ice, Cynthia froze. She gave her niece a long, hard stare as she considered the question. Danita held her breath, waiting. But unlike the rest, she didn't expect a response. The woman was going to mount a defense, so admitting her motivation at this point would be crazy.

"I'm not saying I did any such thing," she told Maya slowly. "But if I did, so what? Your father is a common criminal himself. He's a thief. A liar. He's the man who ruined my Celia's life."

"Mom was happy," Caleb interjected quietly. Brows drawn together, he gave his father a supportive look. "She loved Dad. Loved all of us."

"She could have had anyone. Anything. But she was taken in by the lies." Cynthia turned to face Tobias, arm outstretched as she pointed an accusing finger. "You conned her out of her life just like you conned thousands out of their money. Because of you, she's gone."

Danita met Hunter's gaze with a worried frown. Celia Black had died of leukemia. Did Cynthia really believe her own words? Or was this the groundwork of her defense?

Hunter gave an infinitesimal shrug and moved to take Cynthia's arm again. Clearly, he was ready to end the show.

Cynthia wasn't, though. She pulled away, facing her niece and nephews again as big crocodile tears slid down her cheeks.

"You've all been a delight to me, because you come from my sister. But you can't deny that your father's blood runs through you. All of you. You've emulated his habits, his life choices. I thought you had a chance when you all left him. But you came back. Why didn't you just stay away?"

"Was it easier to set Dad up if we weren't here?" Caleb asked. "Did you think we wouldn't care?"

"I wanted you away from his influence. Living good lives."

"Politically correct lives, you mean?" Caleb corrected. "Why? Dad's career is long and checkered. It's not like making us into pillars of society would distance you from that."

"Oh, please," she dismissed, her usual verve back in place. "If I couldn't spin a criminal in-law into a platform, I didn't deserve to be elected."

"But Dad reformed," Gabriel said slowly. He shook his head as if trying to deny his own words, then lay a hand on the back of his father's chair. "A reformed con artist isn't much of a platform. But a criminal mastermind whose arrest you conveniently oversaw? That'd play great with the media."

She gave a dramatic sigh and shook her head, like her nephew had just stabbed her in the heart, exactly as she'd expected. But she didn't say a word.

"And then there's the sad fact that it costs a pretty penny to play the political game. Doesn't it?" Gabriel gave Caleb a questioning look. "What'd you say? Kill two birds with one stone? Rake in the illegal cash while pointing the finger at the house of cards she built around Dad?"

Cynthia's gasp was just a smidge overdone. Even Tobias, who'd been so silent it was almost like he wasn't there, cringed and shook his head in dismay.

"I've obviously failed Celia," Cynthia said in a tone so hurt, Danita was surprised there wasn't blood leaking all over the floor. "I will be vindicated from this ridiculous accusation. And when I am, you'll regret giving your loyalties to Tobias rather than me."

"It shouldn't be a choice," Caleb said quietly. "If you loved Mom, you'd accept that she loved Dad. If you loved us, you'd accept our loyalty to our father. The only person putting conditions on love is you."

Touched, Danita's eyes met Gabriel's. Did he believe in unconditional love? Was that yet another of those gifts of his heritage? She wanted, so much, to believe it was. And wanted even more to have that for herself.

Needing to get this over with, she stepped forward. Hunter joined her.

"It's time to go now, Ms. Parker," she said, taking the mayor's arm. "Because of your standing in the community, we've arranged for you to be under house arrest rather than in the town's jail until Monday. Two agents are waiting for us there."

Cynthia didn't go quietly. Accusing them all of trying to undermine her political career, Danita and Hunter had to practically drag her to the door.

Unable to stop herself, Danita glanced back. Maya curled at her father's feet, her head on his knee while tears poured down her cheeks. Caleb and Gabriel flanked Tobias's chair.

Danita met Gabriel's eyes. Her lips trembled but she didn't know what to say. Heart shaking at how he must be feeling, she mouthed the word *sorry* before turning away.

This had started as a simple job. Babysit a conman while bringing a crime kingpin to justice and quite possibly bringing down a con artist who'd evaded capture for four decades.

And then it'd turned all upside down. She couldn't even claim that Gabriel conned her out of her heart. Because that, she'd handed to him on a silver platter.

The question was, was it worth her job to get it back?

14

"I SHOULDN'T BE HERE," Danita muttered, smoothing a nervous hand over her long lavender silk skirt. She'd been offering Hunter the same argument all morning and, as he'd done all morning, he kept right on ignoring her. "The case is over. The Black family hardly wants the woman who nearly ruined this wedding playing guest."

Gabriel, especially. If he'd wanted her, he'd have found her. She'd waited, all night, at her room at the inn, hoping he'd show up. That he'd want to resolve things between them, now that the case was over. Before she left.

But he hadn't.

"Relax. You have an invitation and are as welcome here as anyone," Hunter murmured right back as he escorted her down the aisle toward the front of the church. He gave her hand a pat that was more an order than a comfort, followed by "You only have to stay through the toast."

It was a testament to her respect for Hunter—their history and the fact that he was her boss—that she didn't just turn and run.

"Fine. Until the toast," she agreed. And not one second longer, she vowed as she slid onto the glossy bench. Her car was out front, packed and ready to go. If she thought she could get away with sliding all the way across this bench and heading right back up the aisle without Hunter busting her, she'd do it in a heartbeat.

Then the music started. Caleb and Gabriel stepped out of the antechamber together. She sighed a little at the sight of them, so gorgeous and elegant in steel-gray tuxedos, each with a red rose on their lapel.

As if drawn by a magnet, Gabriel's eyes immediately found her. He offered a warm, charming smile that immediately set off her warning radar. Why was he smiling at her? What was he up to? And why did it make her stomach tumble like a giddy virgin?

His gaze narrowed, his eyes heating as they wandered over her. Danita had to force herself not to glance down to make sure her blouse was buttoned.

Then the music changed. With difficulty, Danita tore her gaze from Gabriel's and stood, turning to watch Pandora walk down the aisle on Cassiopeia's arm. Danita was shocked when tears filled her eyes at the obvious love between the two women. Pandora wore traditional white, her gown a vision of froth and lace with a sweetheart neckline and subtle hearts embroidered over the satin. Looking like the Queen of Hearts, Cassiopeia wore a flowing ruby caftan, crystals dangling and roses arranged in her hair.

Terrified to realize that she wanted the same thing—love and marriage and family—Danita fell, rather than sat, back on the pew. The ceremony was a blur as she struggled with the idea of marriage, commitment and all of the possibilities that came with it. Especially as the only person she'd make that promise to would be Gabriel.

When her eyes met his again, she wasn't able to keep all the wishes and hopes in her heart from showing on her face. But instead of looking away, or worse, as if seeing that freaked him out, Gabriel held her gaze. Through the entire ceremony. By the end, her hands were shaking.

She had to get out of here.

As soon as the happy couple made their way back up the aisle, she was out of her seat and heading for the door.

A foot away, a tall figure stepped into her path.

"Danita," Tobias greeted with a big smile. "Let me escort you into the reception hall."

"You don't have to do that," she demurred, trying to find a way to run away and still be polite. He took her arm, though, and led her through the beribboned and flower-strewn hall to the large reception area.

"Please, let me. I'd like to thank you, personally, for everything you did this last week."

She slanted him a look. "For lying to your family, sneaking into your home under false pretenses and exposing an ugly family secret with continued possible legal repercussions?"

"Well, when you put it that way…" he teased, grinning. Gabriel had his smile, she realized with a sigh. "No. Actually, you brought my son home. You cleared my name and you ended an ugly conspiracy that would have hurt a great many people."

Gabriel came by his charm honestly. Her lips quirked. "Well, if you want to put it that way…"

She looked around the reception hall, smiling. Roses draped, hearts flowed. It was an ode to love and Valentine's Day. Then she saw Maya, dressed in red velvet, and a tall, gorgeous blond man. Danita narrowed her gaze. Wasn't he FBI? She was sure he was. She swore she'd aided peripherally in a case he'd worked.

"Maya's engaged to a federal agent?" she blurted out.

"She is. A good guy, that Simon. I'm a proud father. One son an officer-of-the-law, my daughter and other son both planning their future with federal agents. Quite a change for an old troublemaker like myself."

It was like karma coming to Thanksgiving dinner. But that wasn't Danita's concern.

"I'm sorry, but I think you misunderstood what's between Gabriel and me. We only pretended for the case." Swallowing hard against the burning in her throat, Danita tried to pull away. "I should go. I really should."

"Danita, stay." He patted her arm and gave her a look that said he knew she was afraid. "You have a chance at something bigger. At something more lasting than a job well done. Stick around, let me welcome you to our family."

She shook her head. That he wanted her to be a part of the family, after everything, was amazing to her. But despite his skill at manipulating his family, Tobias wasn't calling the shots here.

"I'm sorry," she told him sadly. "But things are over between Gabriel and me."

"Somehow, I don't think so," Tobias said, smiling wide as his glance shifted over her shoulder. With a quick pat to her shoulder, he was gone.

Leaving Danita to take a deep breath and turn to face Gabriel.

"You look good, Blondie," he said, his eyes eating her up like a dieter locked in a chocolate store. "I'm glad you're here."

"Hunter made me," she muttered, not wanting Gabriel to think she'd crash his family's celebration.

"I asked him to."

"Why?"

"We have things to settle." He looked around the hall, festooned with red hearts and white roses, then hooked his arm around her waist. "Let's step out on the balcony."

Needing to know why he wanted her here, terrified

to hope, Danita let him guide her onto the chilly flower-festooned stone balcony. But once there, she stepped away. She had trouble thinking when Gabriel touched her, and she had the feeling she was going to need all her available brain cells for this conversation.

"I like this," he said immediately, running his fingers over the soft cotton of her blouse, a concoction of ruffles and lace that went perfectly with the sedate, ankle-length skirt and old-fashioned kitten-toed boots. "You look sexy."

For the second time, Danita looked down to make sure she was wearing what she thought she was. "Sexy? Yeah, right."

"You do. I like this look. It makes me think of how wild you are in bed."

She resisted the urge to look around and make sure they weren't overheard.

"This is the real you, isn't it?" he asked quietly as his fingers combed through her soft curls. "The person who cares about others, who wants them to be happy. The woman who risks her life for her job, then risk her job for someone she cares about."

Danita swallowed hard, trying to untangle her voice from the fear wrapped around her throat.

"I never said I cared," she finally managed to croak.

"Oh, babe, you care."

All she saw was his cocky smile before he leaned in and took her mouth in his. The kiss was sweet with promise, acceptance and something she was terrified to identify. Her heart said it was love. Her brain screamed at her to not think crazy.

Needing to know, even if it hurt, she reluctantly pulled away from those delicious lips to stare at Gabriel.

"Why?" she asked.

"Why not?"

That cleared the fog from Danita's brain. She gave him

an impatient look, not about to be charmed into sidestepping this discussion.

"Because…" he trailed off, looking over her shoulder at the celebration of wedding bliss. "Because I have feelings for you."

Danita's heart pounded so loud she couldn't hear the music any longer. Hope bloomed. Even though she knew it was crazy. Even though she had no idea how they could make it work, she wanted to try. Wanted to believe that they could have a chance.

"What kind of feelings?" she asked cautiously. What if his feelings weren't as big as her own?

He took a deep breath like a man steeling himself to dive off a burning building and slid his hands into her hair. His fingers cupped the back of her head and he brushed into another soft, sweet kiss. Then he leaned back to give her an intense look that went all the way to the depths of her soul.

"I love you," he said. Before she could do more than gasp, he continued. "I'm quitting the game. I've stashed away enough cash to live a good life while I figure out what to do next. So I'm not asking you to support me or worse, to compromise your beliefs for us to be together. I want to make a life with you. You and me and Pippi. We're all three a little wild, all three used to being on our own. I think the three of us can make a life together, a legal, all on the up-and-up life."

The blood was rushing so fast through her head, Danita could barely hear. All she could do was replay his words over and over as she blinked away tears.

"You're quitting?"

"The cons. The scams. Everything illegal," he confirmed. Then he grinned his wicked grin. "Not the gambling, though. I'm thinking of hitting the professional poker circuit. I'm good, and it'd keep me on the edge so I didn't miss the game so much. But that's legal so it won't mess with your job, right?"

"You're really serious?" Shocked, she could only stare, hoping the words would hurry up and sink in. "You're going to give it all up? I wouldn't have to quit my job?"

Gabriel winced and shook his head. "Oh baby, no. Never. Your job is way too important to you. I love your passion for it, and how damned good you are. I wouldn't mind if you cut back on the hooker jobs, but the rest I'm totally behind."

She laughed. And she believed. He really meant it. They really had a chance.

"I love you," she told him, wrapping her hands around the back of his neck to pull him close for a kiss, trying to put into it everything she felt and couldn't say.

GABRIEL FELT AS THOUGH he was drowning in the delight of Danita's mouth. Pleasure mixed with a relief so strong he could barely stand. Knowing he had to have her soon, he pulled back to finish his declaration of love.

"Look, I'm not very good at this talking thing. Not when it comes to real emotions," he told her quietly. "But I want you to believe me. I want to make sure you give us a chance."

He was a man who'd lived his life taking risks. But Gabriel knew he'd never worried as much about an outcome as he was this one right now.

"Pippi's waiting for us back at the inn. Why don't we go tell her the good news?" Danita said in a husky whisper that sent shivers of desire down his spine. "Then, maybe you can finish this talking about emotions thing while we're both naked."

"I do love you," he exclaimed, laughing. Grabbing her hand, he headed back into the reception hall at a near run. "Let's go."

They made their way through the crowd and across the

room. Just as they reached the door, though, his father called out, "Toast."

Gabriel grimaced.

"So close," he muttered, making Danita laugh in delight. "Just the toast, then we're out of here."

She nodded, her big blue eyes glowing and those full lips, glossy and sweet, curved with joy. This, he realized, was the best game in town. He wasn't going to miss anything else as long as he had Danita by his side.

He accepted two glasses of champagne from the roving waiter, handing one to Danita before wrapping his arm around her again as they turned to watch Tobias raise his glass.

"Welcome and thank you all for joining us today as we celebrate the love and commitment between my son Caleb and his beautiful bride, Pandora."

Ever the statesman, Tobias paused for applause, letting it ring through the room then slowly die down before he continued.

"I'm proud and delighted to welcome Pandora to our family. And I have faith that she and Caleb will carry on the tradition of love and devotion. My only regret is that my lovely Celia couldn't be here to see the culmination of the dreams she had for our children. That they find love. That they embrace happiness. And that they have the strength and devotion to accept commitment and all the work and joy that entails."

Gabriel glanced at his brother with pride. Caleb had done all of that, just like their parents had. Talk about a stellar example.

"To Caleb and Pandora," Tobias continued, "I wish you the depths of love and the breadth of happiness that I had with Celia. May you have years of joy together. Cheers."

A little choked up, Gabriel had to take a few drinks of the bubbly to try and find his voice again.

"Well," he finally said looking at Danita, "there ya go."

He was touched to see the tears glistening on her lashes.

"He really believes, doesn't he?" she whispered, meeting his gaze. "In love. In the power of it?"

"Yeah. He does. And so do I." He set his glass down, then took hers and set it aside, as well, so he could hold both of her hands. Nerves were gone now. He'd never been a man to believe in sure things. But he believed in them now. "I believe in it enough to want to give us a chance at forever."

He watched the nerves fade from her gaze, then a smile spread a glow over her face. "Well, I guess we're both good at taking chances."

"Babe, we're damned good."

BETWEEN JOY AND overwhelming satisfaction, Tobias was sure this was one of the best days of his life. Applause for his toast still ringing in his ears, he stepped from the dais.

"You did it."

He turned to face Rick Hunter, sharing a smile with his old nemesis. Retired from the FBI, Rick had handed down his love for the game to his son.

"*We* did it, actually," Tobias corrected meticulously, tilting his champagne glass so it rang out against his guest's. "I couldn't have brought them home without your help."

"No regrets about the drama surrounding their homecomings? I mean, you had your neck in a noose there for a while."

Tobias's gaze scanned the crowd.

Caleb was dancing with Pandora, his arms curled tight around her as he smiled down into her sweet face. She cuddled close, her cheek resting on his shoulder.

Off in a corner, Maya sat on Simon's lap, her long black curls draped over the hands he'd wrapped around her waist.

The look on his face was pure adoration. He was definitely a man worthy of Tobias's little girl. They talked quietly, both intent upon each other. Planning their future, dreaming of their own wedding.

And Gabriel?

As usual, Gabriel was harder to find. Finally, Tobias's eyes landed on his youngest son. Gabriel had Danita backed up against the door, his intentions clear in the wicked smile he wore. She was shaking her head, but the look on her face was pure love. There was a woman strong enough to handle his wild boy. And good enough to bring out his best side. Just exactly what Gabriel needed.

"No regrets," Tobias told Rick. "My kids are back in my life, and they are all settling into happiness. A man can't ask for a stronger legacy than that."

* * * * *

PASSION

For a spicier, decidedly hotter read—
this is your destination for romance!

COMING NEXT MONTH
AVAILABLE FEBRUARY 28, 2012

#669 TIME OUT
Jill Shalvis

#670 ONCE A HERO...
Uniformly Hot!
Jillian Burns

#671 HAVE ME
It's Trading Men!
Jo Leigh

#672 TAKE IT DOWN
Island Nights
Kira Sinclair

#673 BLAME IT ON THE BACHELOR
All the Groom's Men
Karen Kendall

#674 THE PLAYER'S CLUB: FINN
The Player's Club
Cathy Yardley

You can find more information on upcoming Harlequin® titles,
free excerpts and more at www.HarlequinInsideRomance.com.

HBCNM0212

REQUEST YOUR FREE BOOKS!
2 FREE NOVELS PLUS 2 FREE GIFTS!

Harlequin Blaze™

red-hot reads!

YES! Please send me 2 FREE Harlequin® Blaze™ novels and my 2 FREE gifts (gifts are worth about $10). After receiving them, if I don't wish to receive any more books, I can return the shipping statement marked "cancel." If I don't cancel, I will receive 6 brand-new novels every month and be billed just $4.49 per book in the U.S. or $4.96 per book in Canada. That's a saving of at least 14% off the cover price. It's quite a bargain. Shipping and handling is just 50¢ per book in the U.S. and 75¢ per book in Canada.* I understand that accepting the 2 free books and gifts places me under no obligation to buy anything. I can always return a shipment and cancel at any time. Even if I never buy another book, the two free books and gifts are mine to keep forever.

151/351 HDN FEQE

Name _____ (PLEASE PRINT) _____

Address _____ Apt. # _____

City _____ State/Prov. _____ Zip/Postal Code _____

Signature (if under 18, a parent or guardian must sign) _____

Mail to the **Reader Service**:
IN U.S.A.: P.O. Box 1867, Buffalo, NY 14240-1867
IN CANADA: P.O. Box 609, Fort Erie, Ontario L2A 5X3

Not valid for current subscribers to Harlequin Blaze books.

Want to try two free books from another line?
Call 1-800-873-8635 or visit www.ReaderService.com.

* Terms and prices subject to change without notice. Prices do not include applicable taxes. Sales tax applicable in N.Y. Canadian residents will be charged applicable taxes. Offer not valid in Quebec. This offer is limited to one order per household. All orders subject to credit approval. Credit or debit balances in a customer's account(s) may be offset by any other outstanding balance owed by or to the customer. Please allow 4 to 6 weeks for delivery. Offer available while quantities last.

Your Privacy—The Reader Service is committed to protecting your privacy. Our Privacy Policy is available online at www.ReaderService.com or upon request from the Reader Service.

We make a portion of our mailing list available to reputable third parties that offer products we believe may interest you. If you prefer that we not exchange your name with third parties, or if you wish to clarify or modify your communication preferences, please visit us at www.ReaderService.com/consumerschoice or write to us at Reader Service Preference Service, P.O. Box 9062, Buffalo, NY 14269. Include your complete name and address.

HBI1B

The ruggedly handsome Buckhorn brothers
are back....

Catch both sizzling tales of passion and
romance from *New York Times*
and *USA TODAY* bestselling author

LORI FOSTER

Available now!

"Lori Foster delivers the goods."
—*Publishers Weekly*

**Learn more at
www.LoriFoster.com.**

New York Times *and* USA TODAY *bestselling author Maya Banks presents book three in her miniseries* PREGNANCY & PASSION.

TEMPTED BY HER INNOCENT KISS

Available March 2012 from Harlequin Desire!

There came a time in a man's life when he knew he was well and truly caught. Devon Carter stared down at the diamond ring nestled in velvet and acknowledged that this was one such time. He snapped the lid closed and shoved the box into the breast pocket of his suit.

He had two choices. He could marry Ashley Copeland and fulfill his goal of merging his company with Copeland Hotels, thus creating the largest, most exclusive line of resorts in the world, or he could refuse and lose it all.

Put in that light, there wasn't much he could do except pop the question.

The doorman to his Manhattan high-rise apartment hurried to open the door as Devon strode toward the street. He took a deep breath before ducking into his car, and the driver pulled into traffic.

Tonight was the night. All of his careful wooing, the countless dinners, kisses that started brief and casual and became more breathless—all a lead-up to tonight. Tonight his seduction of Ashley Copeland would be complete, and then he'd ask her to marry him.

He shook his head as the absurdity of the situation hit him for the hundredth time. Personally, he thought William Copeland was crazy for forcing his daughter down Devon's throat.

Ashley was a sweet enough girl, but Devon had no desire

to marry anyone.

William had other plans. He'd told Devon that Ashley had no head for the family business. She was too softhearted, too naive. So he'd made Ashley part of the deal. The catch? Ashley wasn't to know of it. Which meant Devon was stuck playing stupid games.

Ashley was supposed to think this was a grand love match. She was a starry-eyed woman who preferred her animal-rescue foundation over board meetings, charts and financials for Copeland Hotels.

If she ever found out the truth, she wouldn't take it well.

And hell, he couldn't blame her.

But no matter the reason for his proposal, before the night was over, she'd have no doubts that she belonged to him.

What will happen when Devon marries Ashley?
Find out in Maya Banks's passionate new novel
TEMPTED BY HER INNOCENT KISS
Available March 2012 from Harlequin Desire!

USA TODAY bestselling author

Carol Marinelli

begins a daring duet.

THE SECRETS
of
XANOS

*Two brothers alike in charisma and power,
separated at birth and seeking revenge...*

Nico has always felt like an outsider. He's turned his back on his
parents' fortune to become one of Xanos's most powerful exports
and nothing will stand in his way—until he stumbles
upon a virgin bride....

Zander took his chances on the streets rather than spending another
moment under his cruel father's roof. Now he is unrivaled in
business—and the bedroom! He wants the best people around him,
and Charlotte is the best PA! Can he tempt her
over to the dark side...?

A SHAMEFUL CONSEQUENCE
Available in March

AN INDECENT PROPOSITION
Available in April